BREWING A CRUSH

ESAI SANCHEZ

You.

Yes, you.

Repeat after me....

I. AM. WORHTY. OF. LOVE.

Playlist

I Look In People's Windows – Taylor Swift

Am I Enough – Loi

the 1 – Taylor Swift

Unwritten – Natasha Bedingfield

Fix It or Break It – Clinton Kane

This Love (Taylor's Version) – Taylor Swift

I GUESS IM IN LOVE – Clinton Kane

Halo – Caleb Chan, Brian Chan

Fat Funny Friend – Maddie Zahm

Give Me Everything (Stripped) – Archer Marsh

Surrender – Natalie Taylor

better off without me – Matt Hansen

ONE MORE DAY WITH YOU – Clinton Kane

Contents

For those who feel like they are unworthy of love. You are worthy of all great things and love is one of them.

Also, to myself to accept that I'm worthy to be loved and to dream of finding that Heartstopper love.

Chapter One

Leo

I LEAN MY CHAIR back, hovering on two legs, and stretch my neck to see out the window, gazing at the cute stranger who appears to have rented the empty retail space across the street. I've never seen him around Mapleton before. He heaves heavy boxes off the moving truck, one by one, and lugs them through the front door. My chair nearly tumbles over when Nina's voice chimes in my ear.

"Take a picture, it will last longer." She's grinning at me with a raised brow and smirking lip.

"Maybe I should offer to help?" I say and giggle.

"You have been eyeing the new guy ever since you saw him last week. It's giving stalker Leo."

I didn't realize how much I was fixated on the new guy in town. Maybe she's right. I must stop being so desperate for a man who doesn't even know I exist.

"Shut up, Neens," I whisper, as if the stranger could hear me from across the street.

"Grow a pair and say hello to the talk of the town already. Also, please stop calling me Neens. I told you I'm trying to outgrow that childish name you gave me."

She has been trying to get me to stop saying that name for months, but she will always be my Neens. "I'm sorry, that's not happening, *Neens,*" I say with a smirk on my face. "Anyway . . . like it's that simple for a gay man to go up to another man and say 'Hello! I think you're hot and I want you in my pants.' " *I wish.* "Why would I embarrass myself in front of a man like that?"

Neens looks at me with that face I've known my entire life. The expression that warns me that I'm about to get a mouthful. "Leo, I'm saying this in the nicest way possible. This whole 'I'm not good enough or good looking enough' needs to go out the door. You're handsome as hell. If I weren't into women, I would bang you."

My mouth drops to the floor. "Nina Katherine Rose!" I throw a ball of paper, from the box she had set out, at her. "Never in your life say that again Nina. You know I mean it when I use your government name instead of Neens." She throws up her hand in acknowledgement, and I go back to stalking the sexy man across the street.

"Leo, I'm serious. You deserve to find a love worth believing in. Don't count yourself out, okay?"

"I know, I'm working on it okay. Now let's get this table set up with the new books so you can get going."

She is right, I know, but ever since coming out in high school, I've been the only gay man in my hometown that I know of. For years during college, and even after, my family has been trying to set me up with any guy they know to be gay within fifty miles. With my luck, all the guys would have been blind dates, and we may not have made it past the first date. But I rarely get even that far. At this point in my life, all I have time for is the bookstore I took over from my parents. This bookstore has been my haven for as long as I can remember.

Books have been a big part of my life, with my mom being a writer, and my dad being in the publication business. Books are my escape from the reality I have lived for so long. They helped me understand who I was at such a young age. One book in particular gave me the confidence to speak my truth: *Follow the River* showed me the power of what a good story can do for someone's reality.

When the opportunity to be a manager for the bookstore came around, I jumped on it faster than anything. This store is my safe place. I'm glad to make it shine brighter every moment I can. Since becoming an owner, I've started an after-school program where kids of all ages can come hear read-alongs, read by my mother or me.

Being the only openly gay man in Mapleton, I've added representation for the LGBTQ+ community by having more books with queer representation, and inclusive stickers for sale at the front desk. My biggest goal for the store is to be a place where all types of people come to leave life behind. To open a story that will take them away for just a moment, on an adventure they weren't expecting.

We start to set up the New Releases table and it doesn't take long on this typically quiet weeknight. "Neens, it's time for you to get out of here. I'll finish the 'Blind Date with a Book' wall then head out right after."

"Don't say that, because the mall is having a sale right now. Are you sure?" she says to me, already halfway out the door.

I glance across the street. The new owner turned the old sporting-goods store into a very nice-looking coffee shop. Adding plants growing on the brick walls of the old town building has brought out the relaxed vibe, and dark wood tables now sit on both sides of the front entrance, giving customers a place to sit outside. The autumn leaves that fall from nearby trees bring more color to the storefront. He seems to know how to draw people's attention. I haven't noticed anyone leaving or entering the shop, and the lights aren't on. I wonder where the owner is. For reasons I don't understand, my heart is missing the way it feels to see him across the street.

"Leo, get out of your head. You don't even know if he is gay or bi," I whisper to myself.

Whatever his orientation is, it doesn't matter because what are the chances he would want to date me anyway? I kick myself for crushing on someone I've never met. He could be an asshole . . . or smell. I'm romanticizing him in my head based on what he looks like. I don't like people judging me for what I look like, but here I am making assumptions. While I pick up the blind-date books, and add them to the back wall of the store, my mind is racing. I need a distraction. I pull out my phone and put on the comforting playlist I use for the bookstore, and one of my favorite songs flows out of the speakers. Before I can finish putting the books away, I need to set up the small ladder to reach the very top of the wall.

As I reach the top step of the ladder, I hear the chime letting me know someone has entered the store.

"Welcome to Stained Pages, I'll be with you in a moment!" I call out, right as my foot slips on the top step of the ladder. I brace myself for the pain of hitting the hard floor, but instead of feeling the floor, I feel a vibration of heat from someone's touch all around me. It gives me goosebumps.

Someone caught me.

Why was I feeling heat growing in my pants?

"Woah!"

I turn my head to see who has my body in overdrive, looking into deep-blue eyes that have my heart skipping a beat. Those eyes, those ocean blue eyes. I have never felt so safe as with those eyes staring at me with concern. But then it hits me whose arms I'm in and I clear my throat and look away. I get my feet under me, try to stand, and seconds later we both fall to the floor.

Chapter Two

Ryder

MAPLETON, VIRGINIA.

This town will be my new start, and I need it. It's been years since I've been here with my family. Ever since then, I've had this weird bond to it. I've only been here once, when my family and I traveled to see my cousins in West Virginia and our car broke down. We had to stay here for a few days, so we explored the old town. After leaving that weekend it felt like I left a part of my heart here.

"Bossman, where would you like me to put these light fixtures?" a mover says, as I snap out of my daydream.

"Oh umm . . . yeah, you can just set them down near the coffee bar. They're for that area anyway, thank you."

I've always known I would come back here someday, but I never expected to buy an old sporting-goods store and change it to a coffee shop. What makes it even better is that no one knows I moved here a week ago. I wanted a new start, and Mapleton will be that for me.

"Hey Ryder!" I hear from the back of the shop. I turn around to see Jenni coming out of the back room with coffee mugs.

"What's up?"

From this angle of the store, the sun shines its brightest and it makes Jenni look gorgeous. Her dark-brown hair looks lighter with some blonde highlights shaping her face in that perfect model way. Her light brown eyes look like honey when the sun hits it just right. I know I shouldn't be thinking this way about my business partner, but what can a guy do, right?

"Look what came in for the store opening! I think they came out pretty good, don't you think?" Jenni asks as she hands me a hunter green coffee mug that has a logo of a leaf on it.

"They better be, with how much I had to pay for them to be shipped here in time for our Grand Opening." I say sarcastically.

"They are perfect! This will be the best new spot in town Ryder, I know it!"

I admire her positive energy. That's one of the big reasons why I picked her as a partner, other than her having a business degree. I'm just the man with the coffee smarts. I had this dream, but didn't know how to get it started. When I knew I wanted to leave California, I made a listing to find a business partner in Mapleton. Weeks went by with no response. The day I was ready to give up on my dream of moving to Mapleton, my phone lit up with an email notification. The email from Jenni gave me hope that my life was changing for the better. I owe this woman so much; she doesn't even know it.

"Jenni, have I told you how much I love you?" I smile, as I hand the mug back.

"Dude, you've told me at least ten times in the last hour. Are you okay? Do I need to get you some coffee? Better yet, want to get drinks?"

She said the magic words, laughing with a big smile I respond to with no hesitation.

"Drinks sound perfect."

A few hours later, after setting up the shop, I stay back to finish up some cleaning of the entrance before heading out for drinks with Jenni. As I lock up the store, I take a moment to admire what is around me and look at what my new life is going to be like. This shop is my everything and putting my mind into this has been a healing journey so far.

As I look around the downtown street where my shop is located, I notice how out of place my store looks, among all of the office buildings. But across the street, light spills onto the road through a welcoming store window. A bookstore, it looks like. I notice a man working at the front desk, and for a moment I feel this warmth run over me. Something is familiar about him, but I can't tell what. I snap myself out of my pondering and refocus on my excitement on meeting Jenni at the bar.

—-

"How are you feeling princess?" Jenni yells at me, from not even two feet away as I rub my head from the biggest headache I've ever had.

"I'm perfect, thank you very much." I grab a bottle of water and chug it down in a matter of seconds.

"What gave you the bright idea to go out during the middle of the week to have three beer towers?" Jenni asks, as I put my head down on the table to feel some type of stability.

When I met Jenni for drinks last night, one beer tower turned into three. I couldn't stop myself and she didn't try to stop me either, so I turn my head on my arms and just scowl at her.

"You needed to get out of your damn head, Ryder. Plus, it's fun watching you get drunk so easily," Jenni says with the most devilish smirk on her face. I shake my head, laughing at myself. I guess I do not have to worry about her being attracted to me after she saw me sloppy drunk last night. She will be my safe place, my rock here in Mapleton. I'm already very grateful for her.

All day long, I battle my hangover and drink coffee until I feel normal again, while Jenni and I get the shop ready for our Grand Opening.

"It's been a long day, let me finish up here so you can go explore the town more, you've barely left the shop or your apartment since moving here. Don't you want to know the town you moved to out-of-the-blue?"

I never told Jenni about my connection with Mapleton. That story is for me, and me only.

"I guess you're right. It's getting dark, maybe I'll go for a walk or something. The fresh air will do me some good." For a moment my eyes float to the bookstore across the street that I was admiring last night. My eyes may be playing with me, but I swear I saw someone watching me through the store's window.

"Now that sounds like a good idea, Ryder. Go enjoy some well-deserved time off. Now off, get going!" She pushes me around the coffee bar to the door.

"Woah, woah, woah. Let me grab my things first!" I grab my backpack and leave. I take in the cool autumn air, and the rustling sound of the leaves on the sidewalk being blown from the breeze. As I take in the moment, I feel this pull towards something, the same magnetic pull I felt last night when I saw that guy. I cross Maple Drive to the bookstore. As I reach for the door handle, a beautiful girl with long black hair is leaving and almost bumps into me.

"Excuse me! Sorry!" she says as she passes me in a blur.

"Woah! Be careful!" I say.

"My bad!" she calls over her shoulder, clearly in a hurry to get somewhere. She waves and she is gone in the blink of an eye.

The second I'm inside the bookstore, my heart starts thumping and I'm on edge for reasons I don't understand. Then I hear his voice.

"Welcome to Stained Pages, I'll be right with you!"

I look around and see a tan man with curly black hair stepping up a small ladder. He is almost at the top step, reaching out to place a book on a shelf, when I see him slip. Reacting reflexively, I leap forwards, and I catch him before he hits the floor.

"Woah!"

The moment my hands touch him, I felt a burst of heat yet goosebumps run over me. The man turns his head to look at me, and my heart stutters. His eyes shine like the sun is hitting them during golden hour, even if it is dark outside. But what really catches me off guard is how my eyes float to his lips. Lips that call for me to kiss them. Heat was rising within me, and I couldn't help but notice how my dick was throbbing at having him in my arms. Then, as if he could tell I was lost in thought, the man pushes me off, stumbles and we both fall to the floor.

Chapter Three

Leo

It's him.

Why is he here?

Why can't I stop looking at him?

Why did he catch me?

Did he feel how heavy I was?

My mind races as my body hits the ground. My heart is beating faster and faster. *Am I blushing?* My face feels hot. *Does he notice that?*

"Are you okay?" he asks, as I snap out of my daze with the sound of his deep voice.

"Oh umm, yeah . . . I mean, umm . . . yes, ah—thank you for catching me!" *Way to go Leo you sound completely normal.* "I'm sorry for causing us to fall to the ground because you caught me, that's a bad first impression, isn't it?" I giggle nervously as we both get off the floor, but as I put pressure on my ankle it buckles. "Ah, damn it!" He catches my arm to keep me steady.

"Woah, here lean on me. I got you."

There it is again, that sense of vibration the moment his arms are wrapped around me to keep me steady. We lift our heads at the same time as if we are mimicking each other's movements, and our eyes meet once again.

His eyes are so blue, I could get lost in them forever. Wait, is he studying mine too? He clears his throat.

"Let's get you to the front so you can sit down. You may have hurt your ankle from the fall. Let's check it out."

He wraps his arm around my waist, helping me walk to the front as we pass the books lying on the floor from my fall.

"Here, sit down and let me check your ankle," he says to me as he starts to lift my pants to reveal my ankle.

"Oh, um no!" I say awkwardly as I put my hand on top of his. I've always covered most of my body so no one can see how I look. Being overweight for most of my life has done that to me. I especially don't want him to see me like that right off the bat.

"It doesn't hurt that much I promise, you don't need to look at it," I say with a worried smile. With his hand still on my lower leg, he stares at me with this confidence that has my stomach turning, but in a good way. It makes me feel seen and comfortable.

"Don't worry, I won't hurt you; I promise."

I believe him. I lift my hand away from his and let him inspect my ankle.

"Let's see how it looks, okay?"

He lifts my pant leg and rubs my ankle. His touch is softer than what I imagined it would be. He palpates my ankle, trying to see if pressure causes me pain. I notice no pain, thoroughly distracted by thinking of all the other places on my body I want his hands to be.

"It seems like it's not badly sprained. Ice, elevation, and a good night's rest should do the trick."

He looks at me with a smile that takes my breath away. I take a mental picture of how truly beautiful this man is. From his soft chin to his dirty blond hair with a tint of orange. One thing I know for sure is that his eyes will always win me over.

"Thank you for being my hero . . ." Shit, I don't know his name. "Oh, umm, I don't know your name." I laugh awkwardly, putting my hand on the back of my neck.

"My name is Ryder. I'm new in town."

Still kneeling on the ground, he lifts his hand to shake mine. My eyes land on his hand. I study every part of it, his veins, and old scars. I wonder if they are from being burned by the milk steamer or taking food out of the oven. *You're staring, Leo!* I look back up at him and quickly put out my hand to shake. His hand feels rough against my soft fingers, sending butterflies to my stomach.

"I'm Leo, the owner of the bookstore. Welcome to Mapleton, Ryder, it's nice to officially meet the man everyone is talking about." Ryder's face contorts in confusion and his face gets red, as if he doesn't know everyone in town is talking about him.

"Oh, wait, really?" He nervously laughs.

Even his laugh is sexy, what else does this man have that I want?

"Mm-hmm, not a lot happens in this small town, so when someone new comes along, the town buzzes. Especially when that person is *very* good looking." *Oh! Did I just say that out loud?* "Um that's what a lot of girls are saying from what I heard!" I blurt out.

"As long as they come to drink coffee at my shop, they can say whatever they want about me. Did I mention that I'm the coffee shop owner?"

He lifts his head a little gesturing to the store across the street. I refuse to let Ryder know I noticed the minute he arrived across the street, and I've been watching him ever since. I play dumb.

"Really? That's amazing! I did see you move some things earlier last week. I can't wait to have easy access to real coffee other than from the dinosaur of a coffee machine we have in the back room." Honestly, our coffee machine is a very good one, but I'm willing to wake up a few minutes early to get a glimpse of this man in his element.

He smirks at me.

"Well, your first coffee is on the house then. You should come to the opening. Bring your family and friends as well, and if you have a girlfriend, I'd love to meet her."

I laugh out loud.

"No. No, I don't have a girlfriend. Not because I don't want one, it's more that I . . . bat for the other team if you get what I'm saying. I'm gay. No boyfriend for me. But I have a best friend who has been dying for your shop to open, so she will be there." Ryder's face stays relaxed with no sight of judgment. Which is very refreshing to see.

"Ah, I didn't realize, I apologize for just assuming. I'm excited to see what this town has to offer."

I smile back at him with ease.

"No worries, Ryder, it's all good. Thank you again for your help. You saved me from having a sore body tomorrow." My mind slips to the thought of him making my body sore. "Anyway, what brings you to the store other than being a hero?"

His facial expression goes from relaxed to nervous when I ask that question. He starts to clear his throat, his eyes darting around. A book is on the counter, left from when Neens and I were putting new stock away, and he grabs it and hands it to me.

"I came to get this book. I was told it was good and I was passing by after leaving the shop, so I came in to check it out."

I look down at the self-care book and look right back at him.

"You heard it was a good book?" His eyes pinched, chewing his lower lip, he nods, sticking to his statement. "This book was just released today and no one has read this book yet." Giving him a smirk, I giggle. His face turns pale as he looks at the cover of the book, not having realized it had the release date on it.

"I mean, umm . . . yeah, someone told me about it and I guess I assumed they already read it. Maybe I need to stop assuming things, huh?"

I laugh carelessly. I haven't felt this comfortable in a very long time with anyone else other than my parents and Neens. Oddly, I'm enjoying this weird conversation. "It's all good, Ryder. Would you like to get this copy?" He nervously says yes as he messes with his hair. "It's on the house then." I grab the book, tucking in a few bits and pieces, and put it in a tote bag.

"No, no, I can pay for it, Leo, I don't want you to think I helped you just to get something out of it." He tries to hand me money and I refuse. I gesture for him to take the tote.

"Ryder, stop, I'm more than happy to give you this. I added a bookmark that has the store's socials that I run, so give them a follow, and I tossed in a few other little things, please, enjoy them!" I wink at him to be funny, but I don't think he took it as funny. He looks more confused than amused.

"Okay, fine, I'll accept the book if you promise to take care of that ankle." I admire his forwardness.

"Deal!"

I reach my hand out to seal our deal and his eyes float to my hand. It takes him a moment to shake my hand. *Did I freak him out? Great. Way to blow this up, Leo.*

"I forgot some things back at the coffee shop so I'm going to head out," he says quickly.

"I hope you enjoy the book." I don't know what to even think or say. He smiles, nods his head, and heads to the door and my heart starts to ache watching him walk away from me. I turn around to get my emotions in control, but realize I didn't hear the doorbell ring yet. I turn back and my heart skips a beat, Ryder has his hand on the doorknob but he is staring back at me.

"Um, Leo, make sure to take care of the ankle, okay? Don't overdo it, promise?"

I'm stunned.

"I will, I promise, Ryder." A promise I'll keep.

Ryder leaves and my eyes quickly follow his movement to the coffee shop. The way he walks is so calm, yet confident. I want him to turn around and look back at me through the window, but it doesn't happen. I watch as he enters his coffee shop. The door shuts behind him but then opens again. I see Ryder first, but then I see a beautiful woman with dark-brown hair pushing him out the door. They seem to be play fighting. Both smiling big and touching each other. He seems so comfortable with her.

Is he in love with her? Is she his girlfriend? Who is she?

I've seen her around but have yet to learn who she was. The mystery woman turns him around and hugs him and then kisses him on the cheek. My heart sinks. They say their goodbyes and I watch the man who has occupied my mind for days walk down Maple Drive.

Chapter Four

Ryder

IT'S BEEN A FEW days since I met Leo at the bookstore. For some reason, I can't get him out of my mind. Working in the shop has me busy since the opening is only two days away, yet I always have a moment to look out the window to see if he is there working. No luck seeing him though. Is he out of town? Did I not check his ankle correctly? I hope he is okay.

I don't even know this man and I worry about him like I've known him for years. Setting down my coffee mug on my kitchen island I ruffle through my mail. It's mostly junk but an envelope catches my eye, a light blue envelope with no name on it. The postage stamp was from somewhere else, so I don't know what to think. Maybe it was a mistake, and for someone else in my building. I put it aside, grab my mug, and head to the patio.

The best thing about this apartment is that it's all mine. It's an old factory building and the red bricks pop out. With the floor being a nice dark wood tone, it matches the rustic vibe of the town. I did well with finding a good home for myself. The only thing missing is someone sharing it with me. Opening the sliding door, I take in the cool morning air and take a deep breath in. Breathing out, I let go of all my worries and stress of the day and focus on what my day can be.

My building is not too far from the town square, giving me a glimpse of Mapleton as its day begins. The sky shines bright colors of orange, yellow, and purple as the sun rises. Leaves rustle from cars driving by as I watch residents get ready for their workday, and kids get on the bus to go to school. This town amazes me in so many ways, with its sense of unity, and a calmness that strikes me so well. Most importantly what it gives me is stability, and that's what I need the most right now. I hear a faint alarm sound going off in the kitchen, warning me that it's past seven and that I need to get ready to go to work. I take one last look at Mapleton, my new home. Smiling as I slide the door closed to start my day.

"Ryder! Did you hear me!"

I jump, startled out of my thoughts, and drop the mug in my hand with a loud crash. "Shit!" I hear footsteps rushing towards me as I bend down to grab the broken mug from the floor.

"Are you okay? What happened?" Jenni asks with a worried expression.

"Ah, nothing. I just . . ." My eyes float to the store across the street again where they were a few moments ago. "I bumped into a table. My bad, you called for me?" I ask Jenni and she follows my gaze to what I was looking at.

"Yeah, I've been calling you for the past five minutes. Are you sure you are good?"

My gaze falls back on her.

"Mm-hmm, for sure, what do you need?" Her face scrunches up as she looks at me and then the street.

"I've noticed you've been distracted and looking at the bookstore across from us a lot. Why's that?"

Damn it, have I been doing that a lot?

I laugh nervously.

"Oh, have I? I guess I forgot to tell you, I met the owner of the bookstore the day you told me to leave early to relax. I kind of caught him when he was falling." My face contorts into confusion.

"What do you mean 'when he was falling', Ryder?"

I smile. "It's kind of funny, I was walking in and as he was stepping up on a ladder he slipped, and I caught him before he fell. Then we talked for a little while and I got a book before I left." Okay, a lot more happened, but she doesn't need to know all that.

"Oh, okay, well that was nice of you. But that doesn't answer my question of why you have been looking over there nonstop." She's determined to get an answer from me.

"I told him about the opening of the coffee shop. He mentioned that people have been chatting about me, so I want to make a good impression, you know?" Okay, that's a good enough answer for sure. She nods her head taking in my answer. I do wonder what people have been thinking about me. I hope they will like me.

"Talk around town is good for business. Did you tell him when it was? The opening I mean."

"Oh shit!"

Jenni laughs as I realize I never told Leo when the coffee shop opens.

"I assumed you didn't, typical Ryder. Well, go tell him after we get this work done. We have some interviews with potential employees." I nod and follow her to the back room.

As the interviews start, all I think about is the next time I get to see and talk to Leo. Whenever I had a moment to look away, my eyes floated to the bookstore, hoping he was there. Jenni has these interviews down, so I'm not paying any mind unless I need to.

I wait till we finish an interview to whisper to Jenni "Hey, do you mind if I step out for a moment?"

She nods her head, not fully paying attention.

I get up from the table and push my chair in. My heart starts racing, knowing I'll get to see Leo in a matter of minutes. The man that has me in a daze. I don't even bother to take off my apron as I head out the door and walk to the stoplight. I take a moment to myself to look around and take in the moment, from the cars passing by to the colors of the autumn leaves flying with the breeze. The crossing light turns white, signaling that I can walk, but as I take my first few steps—eyes glued to the window hoping to see Leo—I hear someone shouting.

"Watch out!!" I hear, as a biker zooms past me and I trip backward, falling on the road.

"Damn it!" I let out as the biker stops a few feet away from me.

"Are you okay dude!? You need to watch where you are walking!"

I turn to wave a hand at him letting him know I'm okay. He gets on his bike and starts riding away. As I get up, I rub off dirt and rocks that are embedded into my hands.

"Get off the road!" a driver screams out their window at me.

I safely get to the other side and check myself for injuries. Once I know it's nothing more than a few scrapes I try to compose myself.

Even though the autumn air is cold, I feel this fire all around me. I turn around and my eyes meet a set of light brown eyes that I have been craving for.

Chapter Five

Leo

"So, TELL ME MORE about how you and Ryder met because this is giving rom-com, Leo!" Neens blurts out as she walks back to the front.

"Shhhh! There are people in here, stop yelling!" I say, as I put my finger to my lips to make sure she got the idea.

Giggling and giving me devilish eyes she walks up to me, bumping me with her elbow. "Well, it's the most action you've gotten in months, Leo. I think it's something worth talking about." I shove her back as we both laugh at her joke.

"First off, there was no *action* involved. He helped me with my ankle, okay? That's all." I turn my head in the direction of the coffee shop.

"Oh, so does that make him your hero now? Your sexy hero." Neens puckers her lips, making a kissing noise.

"Nina, shut up. Stop making fun of me. I told you about Ryder because I needed to tell someone, not be made fun of, okay?"

"Leo, I'm playing around." Nina laughs and tries to move in for a hug. I put a hand on her shoulder to stop her.

"Don't touch me." With determination in her eyes, she pushes my hand off and rushes to hug me. I let her because she is my person and I can't be mad at her.

I feel Nina's body tense up and I break our embrace. Her eyes drift outside, and we see Ryder striding across the street, coming this way. My heart starts to race. There he is, looking so sexy my heart can't handle the way it's beating for him.

"Is he coming over here?" Neens wonders.

"I don't know, he could be going for a walk, but why is he wearing his work apron?" My eyes scan every inch of him. The way his black t-shirt fits, and his biceps grow bigger when he moves his arm to touch his hair.

"Oh fuck!" Neens yelps, as a biker zooms past Ryder and he falls hard on the ground.

"Woah! What the hell was that biker thinking? Ryder could have gotten hurt!" I rush around the front counter to get to Ryder, but Neens grabs my arm.

"No Leo, I think he is okay. He just got up and cleaned himself off."

I stop my mad charge out of the store and watch with Neens, as Ryder makes it to the sidewalk. With one hand I rub absentmindedly at my chest as my pulse steadies.

He's okay.

He stops near the light post and starts to regain his composure. I secretly hope he comes to see me. My body feels this heat that I still can't under-stand. As if he read my mind, he turns around and somehow our eyes meet. For a moment it feels like nothing is around us and all I care about is feeling him on my body.

"Leo! He's coming in, act normal!" Neens whisper shouts.

"Fuck! Move over dude!" I shove Neens to the counter and grab a book to open to make it look like I'm doing something other than staring at him. The doorbell rings open.

"Hello, welcome— Oh, Ryder! Hey, what's up dog?"

What's up dog! What the actual hell is wrong with me?

Neens shakes her head at me and covers her face. Ryder laughs at me, at least he thought me calling him "dog" was funny.

I rub the back of my neck nervously. "I mean, what's up?" I ask as I clear my throat. "Are you okay? Are you hurt? We saw that you fell outside. I have a med kit if you need one." I babble as I reach below the counter.

"No, no, I'm fine other than being *extremely* embarrassed. You saw all that?" He messes his hair with one hand, blushing slightly. Maybe it's a nervous tic, and what a cute one it is.

"I was coming over to tell you, the grand opening of the coffee shop is in two days. You should come."

Ryder looks so adorable when he puts his hands in his pockets and starts rocking back and forth on his heels.

"I'll be there, Ryder." I confirm with a soft smile.

Out of the corner of my eye, Neens catches my attention by air-humping the wall trying to be funny. A I want to do is throw a book at that idiot, but Ryder laughs at Neens.

"Let me formally introduce you. Ryder, this is Neens. Neens, this is Ryder," I gesture to both, and they smile.

"It's nice to officially meet you, Neens."

"Yeah, no, don't call me that ever again," she smirks and Ryder looks stunned. "Mister Leo here has been calling me that since we were both young and, since he's my best friend, I allow him to be the only one to say that name. So, to you I'm Nina, okay?" She winks at him, and I feel my lunch wanting to come back up.

Ryder laughs. "Well, I'm glad to meet the famous best friend Leo told me about." Turning to me, he adds, "Leo, please bring this lovely girl to the opening with you, okay?" Then he winks at me and I freeze.

The things this man makes me feel. I don't know how to process it all.

"I got to head back. I'm supposed to be doing interviews, but I was thinking about you and wanted to check in." His face gets red and he looks like he's just realizing what he said. "Umm yeah . . . have a good rest of your day guys!" He turns around so fast it's like a blur and practically runs out of the store. The door hadn't even closed by the time he crosses the road. Okay, the first thing to teach him is road safety.

As the coffee shop door closes behind Ryder, Neens and I look at each other. She opens her mouth to say something but I stop her.

"Nope, don't say a thing."

She opens her mouth, "But—"

I put my hand up. "I said no. End of discussion."

She bursts out laughing and goes to walk past me then, over her shoulder, with a completely straight face, she says "What's up . . . *Dog.*"

"Oh my—" I grab a book to throw and she runs to the other side of the store as I follow.

Chapter Six

Leo

EVER SINCE RYDER VISITED the bookstore, my anxiety has been coming in waves. Now it's the day of his opening, and I'm freaking out. I know that we can't be anything more than friends. Who wants to date someone who looks like me? I'll admit, I have a cute face for a fat guy, but I'm not good enough to be anyone's boyfriend.

Looking through my closet, I mentally consider and discard shirt after shirt. Nothing fits me the way I wish it did. I can't work out why I care so much about how he views me. I've learned to block out these emotions years ago, when I was very young. Being friends with Neens, it was hard growing up and I'm not blaming her. I've been known as her 'ugly fat friend' since elementary school. People would make fun of me whenever she wasn't around, calling me her pet and picking on my appearance. But without her, I don't think I could have made it to this age. For years I've picked on myself, thinking I could get stronger by accepting who I was: the fat ugly friend.

I stare at my reflection in the mirror and look at every imperfection staring right back at me. The jeers and laughter of a lifetime of bullies echo in my head. I can't escape these emotions. I've tried so many times, but these feelings find their way back, at the worst times to hurt me more and more. What makes it worse is knowing that I'm the one who hurts my own heart.

I throw the shirt I had in my hand across the room and grunt with frustration.

Sitting on the edge of the bed I put my hands over my face and try to focus on my breath. I'm drowning under a sea of negativity, and all I can do is try to breathe slowly as I cry. Through the rushing in my ears, I hear a knock on my bedroom door and then hear it open.

"Hijo estas bien? Te escuche gritar."

I look up with wet eyes and see my mother looking at me with worry.

"Oh my—Leo, what's wrong? What's happening?" She rushes to my side and hugs me.

My mother has always been my biggest supporter, through thick and thin. When I came out in high school, she just looked at me and smiled. She didn't question me about anything and got up to give me one of the freest hugs I've ever felt. With that embrace, all my worries disappeared. She was by my side when I came out to my father—who also took me in with hugs and kisses.

I have the best parents and I'm very grateful for them. Not everyone has this type of support and that's why I cherish them with my entire being.

Rubbing a tear off my cheek, I look into her eyes. "I'm okay. I promise. I just got too in my head about something."

She smiles softly

"Tell me what's going on, hijo. I don't see you get this upset unless it's something big."

She's right. I don't let these emotions get to me as much as they did when I was younger.

"Well, there's this guy . . . and I know there is no chance in hell anything would happen. I know that. But for some reason it has me feeling so unlovable. My head is spinning with so many dark thoughts about myself and how I look. I like him, but I know someone like him won't like someone like me." I'm gesturing to my body and face as I talk.

My mother just fixes me with a look that comforts me in a matter of seconds.

"Leo, look at me when I tell you this, because I'm serious. You, my son, are one of the sweetest, hardworking, handsomest, and bravest men I've ever met in my lifetime. I'm not just saying this because I'm your mother, but as a person on this planet. who has seen you struggle with these emotions and anxiety. You have proven—to not only me but many others—that you are more than what you look like. You are more than love itself. You are you. Someone who I'll fight for, time and time again."

Face filled with tears, I look at my mother, smiling with so much joy that all I can say, with a big exhale of relief, is "Thank you."

"I'm assuming this boy is the new coffee shop owner?" she asks, as she smirks at me.

I laugh, rubbing away the tears from my cheeks. "How did you know?"

"Baby, I'm your mother. I'm not dumb. I've seen how you keep looking out the bookstore window during your shifts. I put two and two together when I saw him looking across the street one afternoon, as I was closing the store. It seemed like he was looking for you."

I get up from the bed so fast at that, my head rushes, "Wait! What? What do you mean he was looking for me?"

She giggles as she gets up and heads out the door.

"No! Mom! Tell me!" I say frantically, following her out of the room, where she stops and turns towards me

"Nope. Now get ready. Nina should be here soon and we can head to the opening, okay?"

I nod and go back to the closet to look for an outfit. I have the perfect one in mind.

Neens arrives at the house later than expected. Walking to the coffee shop with with her and my mother, I check the time as we approach, then elbow her side. "Nina, I swear I told you I wanted to get there when it started and now we're an hour late."

"Ouch! Dude, I'm sorry I was dealing with a makeup emergency! I had to run to the store across town, okay?" Typical Neens. Of course it was because of makeup.

"Whatever you say, Nina . . ." I huff, as I roll my eyes at her.

"Hey! Stop using my government name, Leo!"

I smirk, "I thought you *wanted* me to start calling you by that name, am I right?" She looks at me and we both start laughing loudly.

"Now that's the two best friends we like to see." My father's voice sounds behind me and I turn mid-laugh to my parents.

"Hey Dad, thought you weren't coming?" I comment.

"I wasn't going to but then I saw how busy the coffee shop was getting. I closed the store a little early to come join you guys."

He smiles at me and leans in for a hug. My dad has always been the provider of the family. When he found out that my mother was pregnant with me, he decided to leave the office he was working at to stay closer to my mother and me once I was born. Not long after I was born, they came up with the idea for the bookstore and started it while my father worked remotely with his old company for a few years. He inspires me to work hard to achieve all my dreams. My parents' love is pure and strong. I hope to have half of what they have one day.

"Let's get going, I need a double blonde shot," he comments, waving us on. "Your mom needs her fix of mocha as well. Right, sweetie?" he asks, kissing my Mom on the cheek.

"Mm-hmm, I do need it. I was up late writing again."

She's been writing this book that she won't let anyone know about. It's frustrating. She's a hella good writer and I really want to know what this book is about.

"Sooo, Mom . . . what's the story about?" I ask quickly, trying to see if I could trick her into giving me any details.

"Nope. Sorry not sorry, hjio."

Well, that didn't work.

They pass me and Neens on the sidewalk as I admire how amazing they look together, even now. I don't know how I'm the mix of the two of them because all I seem to have from them is my mom's black curly hair and my dad's dark tan skin.

We arrive at the coffee shop to find Dad was right: it's packed with locals. Ryder was worried for nothing. His shop is a huge success.

"Wow. This is crazy! Look at all the people. Was it like this when you opened the bookstore, Mr. and Mrs. Blanco?" Neens asks my parents.

"When we first opened it wasn't as big as this, but it was very memorable." My mother replies, as we join the back of the line waiting to go into the shop.

"What is the owner's name again, Leo?" my father asks me.

"It's Ryder. I believe he is around my age."

Waiting in line, my eyes float to the brick wall, with green leaves and vines wrapping around like a spider web. Turning to see how easy it is to look at the bookstore from this spot, I notice the light post right outside, wreathed in leaves as well. I smile at the thought of having something connecting our stores like an unexpected bond.

I turn as we enter the shop door and, as I walk in, my breath catches as I lay my eyes on Ryder. He is wearing his navy-blue apron with *The Coffee Crush* and their leaf logo on it. Under it, his white t-shirt fits him like a glove in all the right places, showing off his muscles perfectly. His blue jeans make his ass look like Captain America's. My eyes slowly gaze at every inch of this sexy human, from his denim-clad calves to his broad shoulders, his strong neck, his soft chin. His hair is styled perfectly, except for a few pieces falling in his face, and his eyes seem bluer than ever, shining so bright from the lights in the shop. My heart thuds, from excitement or nerves, I couldn't tell. Then Ryder spots me, and everything stops as he looks at me with the biggest smile and waves.

"Leo, you're here!"

I wave back and smile.

Chapter Seven

Ryder

IT'S THE DAY OF my opening. I've been waiting for this chance for so long, and it's finally here. *Why can't I control my anxiety?* I'm scared thinking something is going to go wrong and that I'm going to fail again. My life hasn't been going the way I wish it would. Leaving California was my ticket to freedom, but did the negative energy follow me? Taking a deep breath, I start counting to ten and I slowly exhale all the bad thoughts. As my head floats to a space where I feel in total control, I think of a set of light-brown eyes that make my heart swarm with happiness. *Leo.* Slowly and surely, he has become a way for me to get my emotions in control, my measure of what it feels to feel safe and supported. I open my eyes and in that moment I'm ready to get this day started.

My red Jeep is the one thing that I'm glad to have from California. This Jeep has been my escape when I needed it the most. The views in California are hard to beat, but I hope next summer I can visit some spots to enjoy here in Mapleton. I heard there's a lookout on a lake that I would love to check out soon.

Driving through town in my Jeep, seeing all the life that this town is breathing, always brings comfort to my heart. I watch a couple walking together near the town square, holding hands, enjoying each other's company, and all I think about is what life could be like if I gave someone a chance.

Leo. What would it be like to be with him? Not a lot of people know that I'm bisexual. It's my business and no one else's until they need to know. I've only dated girls and had a few casual hookups with guys at parties. I didn't explore more with any other guy because there's this one guy I met so long ago, that my heart is waiting for. I don't know if I could love anyone right now.

Snapping out of my thoughts, I turn onto Maple Drive. I see a long line outside my shop and my heart screams excitedly. I park the Jeep and rush to the back door to meet with Jenni to get the shop open.

"Ryder!! Are you ready!? The day is finally here!"

"I'm honestly riding high, but we have no time. We need to get these doors open. Get the crew together so we can chat before we open."

She gathers everyone in the back as I get my apron on and wash my hands, grinning at myself in the mirror.

It's official: I'm running my own coffee shop.

"Hey everyone! I wanted to say a few words before we start this crazy journey. First, thank you for being a part of this dream of mine. You were all selected due to your amazing personalities and I know you'll be the perfect crew for this shop. I want to shout out to my amazing business partner, Jenni! Without you, I don't know where I'd be right now. You helped me achieve this dream. For that, I'll always be grateful. Now let's get going!"

With so much pride, I unlock the door and the first ring of the doorbell starts this journey.

"A large caramel macchiato with blonde shots upside down for Cece!" I hear from the coffee bar as customers come in and out the doors. Coffee has been my obsession for the longest time, so today was the perfect day to make drinks and spark connections with customers. We've been busy since the door opened, but in the back of my mind, I keep waiting for that one person to walk in the door. Every time I hear the door chime, I look up as I make drinks, hoping it will be him, but as the day goes, my heart gets a little less hopeful. I check the clock to see how long it has been since we opened and it's been almost two hours. *He will come. He has to.* I try to stay focused on being a good business owner and taking care of the customers.

"This is a beautiful place young man! The coffee is delicious. You will do amazing!"

I lift my head and an older couple is looking at me with the biggest smiles, takeout cups in their hands. I smile, thanking them for the support. "Please don't be shy and visit again! This shop is for everyone to enjoy."

The older man starts to laugh as he looks at his wife.

"Don't tell her that because she will take you up on that and never leave." She bumps him with her elbow, as he takes a sip of coffee, making him spill a little.

"Don't listen to my husband, he thinks he is a comedian. Honey, you will do amazing things here I know it! Congratulations!"

My heart fills with joy as I give them the biggest smile, "Thank you to you both. My name is Ryder. As of right now, you both are my first regulars!"

"Oh honey, that is so sweet! We are the Johnsons. It's a pleasure to meet you and never feel scared to reach out. We will leave you to it, Ryder. Enjoy this day!" They wave as they walk out the door.

The door chime sounds as I'm busy making a drink. As soon as I pass the drink down the line, I feel this heat and look up.

There he is. Leo.

Without even thinking I shout out, "Leo, you're here!" and wave at him with excitement.

My heart starts to flutter at how handsome he looks, in a pale mint button up with the sleeves rolled up. The first four buttons are open, showing off his white t-shirt and a silver chain. His neck looks so good I want to just bite it and kiss it gently. His blue jeans are loose, yet fit him so well that the view of his ass from this angle drives me crazy. I can't stop looking. He fits the whole bookstore owner vibe with this outfit and I'm loving every inch of him right now.

"Hey Jenni, I'm going to take a sec, I'll be right back," I pass by her at the register.

"Sure, don't worry about it, I think we got it here. Go be a good owner and mingle with customers."

I nod and head towards the man who has my hands sweating. "Hello everyone! Thank you so much for coming! It means a lot."

I know Nina, but the other two people with them I can only assume are Leo's parents.

"Hello, young man! It's a pleasure to be here. I'm Paul and this is my beautiful wife, Elena." He gestures to the woman that looks to have Leo hair, and I notice his eyes are familiar, but not quite the same as Leo's. These are definitely Leo's parents.

"You're Leo's parents—I can tell where he got his looks from," I smirk at him, seeing Leo's face go red as he and Nina exchange glances.

"Oh, you're too kind! You're very handsome yourself. Ryder, correct?" his mother asks, as Leo's eyes grow wide.

"Mom!" he whispers to her.

I laugh at the exchange and enjoy the moment.

"Yes ma'am, it's Ryder." I offer my hand, but she pulls me in for a hug.

"We are a hugging family, Ryder, so no handshake, okay? Nina knows the rules, right?" Nina giggles at this, nodding. I love how easy it is with them. I'm never usually good with parents, having not had the best example growing up.

"Let's get you guys some drinks! What are your orders, I'll get them going. I told Leo that your drinks are on the house due to our deal from the other day."

His mother looks at him with confusion.

"What deal, Leo?" He looks at her, and then at me, then back at her.

"Oh umm, yeah, what had happened was, I was setting up the blind book dates on the wall and I slipped off the step ladder and Ryder was there to catch me," Leo babbles. "I hurt my ankle and he helped me to the front when I couldn't walk. So in return, I gave him one of our new books and, in exchange, he offered to give us free coffee to make it fair."

His mom's face softens, as she looked at me and smiles.

"Thank you for helping my son, Ryder. It means the world to me that someone takes care of him. Don't be shy. Come over whenever you like, okay?" She leans in for a mother hug and I embrace it, marvelling at how she made me feel safe in a matter of minutes. Leo is lucky to have these two amazing people. I would be blessed to have them in my life too. I hope I can. I smile and look at Leo, "I'll always be there to help"

We stare into each other's eyes like the very first time at the bookstore.

Nina clears her throat, breaking the awkward silence. "So, can I get my coffee now or what?" she asks.

I chuckle, turning towards her. "Just order upfront and we can get them ready for you." I turn back to Leo, noticing how he hasn't kept his eyes off me. *He makes me feel so good.* "Leo, what's your order?"

He takes a moment to look at the menu, rubbing the back of his neck in the cutest way. I could watch him all day long.

"I'll take a, ummm . . ." He looks confused, but then his gaze comes back to me and he smiles. "Make me your favorite drink."

"Perfect choice. It'll be right up."

Chapter Eight

Leo

THERE IS SO MUCH to do, and I have no time for it. I've been so wrapped up in Ryder, I completely forgot about the town's block party. It's also my birthday in a week, for which I have no plans, but that's not important right now. My parents *finally* gave me the responsibility of running the booth at the annual block party, which means so much to me and will hopefully show my parents I'm ready to take on more for the store. But I have no idea what to do for the booth.

"Hey my love, how's sales today? I'm looking at our sales from last year."

I look up from my computer to see my mom across from me looking at the store's paperwork.

"Let me check quickly. Sorry, I'm not thinking straight."

"You okay? Where's your head at?"

I don't want to worry my parents, but I think it's best to confide in them.

"Yeah, I am. Well, I'm struggling with the booth for the block party this year. This is my first year doing it on my own. I want to prove to you guys that I can handle this." Rubbing my temples I take a deep breath.

"Papa, it's okay. Don't let yourself overthink anything. I know you will handle this with ease. That is why we know you are ready for this. You will do something amazing, I know it."

"Thanks mom, I hope to make everyone proud."

"You will Papa! Now what are the numbers."

I print out the numbers for today's sales and give them to her.

"They are looking good so far! Okay, let's get some stuff stocked."

We're so distracted we don't hear the doorbell ring, and I jump as I realize Ryder is standing in the store, watching us with a small smile.

"Ryder! Hello, you surprised us! It's so nice to see you here. Sorry for the lack of attention," my mother says, going in for a hug.

I study Ryder's face as he gives my mother a one-armed hug. *He's so beautiful.*

"Hello to you as well Mrs. Blanco! It's always a pleasure seeing you."

"What brings you to our shop today?" she asks, elbowing me on the side.

"I wanted to drop this off for Leo." He holds up a takeout cup that looks like the same drink he made me on the day of the opening.

"How did you know that I've been craving this? I'll admit, I don't drink coffee often, but this is amazing."

What made him think about bringing me this drink?

"At first I didn't know if you liked it due to it not being coffee."

"Wait? This isn't coffee? Then what is it?" Honestly, I don't care much about the drink, but more about the hands that made It.

"It's a green tea drink where I add steamed milk and let it brew for a few minutes, letting the flavors soak in the milk. This time I added coconut milk to make it a little sweeter, like you." He winks at me as he hands me the drink, then adds, "What was that I was hearing about a block party and a booth?"

I slightly choke as I take a sip. Just how long was he listening?

"Yes!" my mom jumps in to answer. "Mapleton's block party is an annual event for businesses in Mapleton to be showcased at and celebrate the community. Since most owners are so busy with their work, they never get the chance to enjoy some of the town's fun festivities. This gives them the chance to do just that, but also introduce something new for their store."

Damn, Mom let me speak.

Interrupting Mom when she finally takes a breath, I add, "Exactly what my mom said, but the one thing that makes the block party fun, is that each store has to bring something new every year and there are prizes for the best ideas. It can get competitive, that's for sure. Last year, the sports store won by having a mini golf course kit for little kids to use in the house. This year, I'm going to bring home the gold."

"As you can tell, Leo is very passionate about this year's booth," my mom chips in. "We are giving him the chance to run the booth, while his father and I enjoy the party for once. However, it is stressing him out too much. Why don't you get him out of his head, Ryder?"

Did she just . . .? I give my mother the shadiest stare as she walks away from the front.

"You don't need to help me with anything I—"

He stops me mid-sentence, "Leo, it would be my honor to help you with this. I didn't get to go to anything like this growing up and it would give me the chance to see how things could go when my shop can join."

"Are you sure? Aren't you still busy, with the store just opening?"

"I can handle it! I have my crew, and my partner Jenni there to support me. Let's meet up soon and we can do some brainstorming. I want this year to be your year!"

I don't know what to even feel right now. *Is he flirting with me? Is he just doing this to be nice? Or is there more to this?*

I can't handle all these questions buzzing round my head. I have too much riding on this booth. What harm could a little help cause, right? "Deal, then!"

"Deal it is Leo! Let's make it official." He raises his hand as if to shake mine but stops. "I'm going to take a page out of your mom's book."

He walks around the counter, and before I have time to think, he has his entire body embraced with mine in a hug.

Ryder is hugging me! What should I do?

I awkwardly pat his back, as I take in the warmth from his body and lean into the comfort it brings over me. Breathing deeply, I take in the scents that make up Ryder. His cologne gives off wood tones and a little hint of a floral scent. But the one scent that I know will always be on him is freshly ground coffee.

I think I'm going to start liking the smell of coffee more and more.

"I like this way of making deals a lot better, don't you?" I giggle, letting go reluctantly.

He laughs as we break our hug and messes with his hair, ducking his face and blushing slightly.

"I agree with you there. I'll leave you to your brainstorming then. But I'll see you soon. Yeah?"

Smiling from ear to ear I reply, "Yes, it's a date."

Wait, did I say that?

"It's a date."

Before I can take back what I said, he is gone as quickly as he came in.

Chapter Nine

Ryder

That's what he said, right? I don't know, but my mouth was working all on its own when I answered back. I rushed out of there so fast before I realized I didn't have a way to contact him.

Lying in bed all I could think about was wanting to talk to Leo, but don't know his number. Then it hit me. He runs all the social media accounts for the store!

"Where is that card?" I whisper to myself, getting out of bed.

Searching the room trying to find the bag with the book he gave me. No luck.

"Oh shit! It's in the Jeep!" I quickly get dressed, get the keys and head to the parking lot.

I look in the back seat and there's the bag from the bookstore. Taking it back inside, I empty the contents onto my bed. Tucked into the front of the book I had randomly chosen is a card with all the store's information on it.

Instagram seems the easiest way to contact him, so I pull out my phone and open the app. I type in "StainedPagesBooks" on the search bar and watch all the accounts pop up. The top profile picture shows a light post shining during a winter storm, but what made me know it was the right account was the leaves wrapping around the snow-topped pole.

It's what I expect from a business account, with book sales and promotions posts mostly. I keep on scrolling, trying to find any sign of Leo. Post after post of nothing much, until . . . there! I click on the post and what pops up takes my breath away. It's a photo of Leo reading a book, near the window of the store during golden hour. He looks relaxed with his tan skin glowing perfectly in the soft sunshine and curls falling in front of his face. My eyes scan every bit of him I can see in the photo, then I notice something in the background. Looking closer, I see my shop window was reflecting the sun towards Leo.

Were we always meant to be in each other's lives?

Or am I just overthinking?

I smile, my body heating at the thought, and click to save the photo. I hit follow and send a message.

> @Coffeecrush13: Hello, from one owner to another.

> @Coffeecrush13: That sounded weird, sorry!

> @Coffeecrush13: Hi, this is Ryder. I sorta forgot to ask for your number when I left, but you gave me the store's card. So here I am!

@StainedPagesBooks: Ryder!

@StainedPagesBooks: I was thinking the same thing. I was planning to come see you tomorrow, but looks like you beat me to it. Loved that you used the card I gave you to find me.

@Coffeecrush13: Great minds think alike right?

@Coffeecrush13: I hope I didn't bother during a bad moment. I wanted to talk about when we can meet to run some ideas for the booth.

@StainedPagesBooks: Not a bother at all! You are saving me from the embarrassment of my parents singing old Spanish songs with Nina's parents. We do these weekly dinners, and every time it ends with them drunk singing from all the tequila they had during dinner.

@StainedPagesBooks: Nina was supposed to be here but left me to go on a date -.-

@Coffeecrush13: Well, that's not fair at all.

@Coffeecrush13: Sounds like you need a hero again! Want to meet up?

@StainedPagesBooks: what do you have in mind?

> @Coffeecrush13: you up for a night drive around the town?

> @StainedPagesBooks: I think that sounds like a perfect plan. Anything to get me away from these monsters of singers lol.

> @Coffeecrush13: Meet at the light post in front of your store? I'll drive.

> @StainedPagesBooks: Yeah, that's perfect. I'll get ready.

> @StainedPagesBooks: See you soon Ryder!

> @Coffeecrush13: See you soon!

Well, that took a different turn than how I thought it would go. But, at least I finally get some alone time with Leo, to see where these emotions go.

I hop out of bed and head to take a quick shower since I went to the gym earlier. I don't need Leo to think I stink, and with the scent of coffee on me every moment of the day, sweat and coffee do not need to mix.

Windows down, with air blowing through my hair, I drive to the bookstore smiling. The closer I get to the store, the tighter my chest feels, yet I feel like I'm able to breathe better.

I pull onto Maple Drive and notice the shining light at the end of the street. Standing next to the light pole is Leo, wearing a baby blue hoodie with gray sweatpants.

Now I understand the obsession of men in gray sweatpants.

They cling to his thick thighs and round ass, leaving just enough to the imagination to be perfect.

My palms start to sweat a little. I don't get anxious much nowadays, but since meeting Leo, my body has been acting all types of weird.

"Hey, stranger!" I say, as I pull up next to Leo.

"Hey!"

I turn on the hazard lights and get out of the car, stepping up right in front of Leo. Ever since I met his mom all I want to do is give hugs out. To Leo, most importantly.

"Hey," I whisper.

"I think you already said that." He giggles, making me feel warmer inside.

I laugh, "I think you're right, but your mom taught me a very important life lesson."

"And what is that, Ryder?"

With one hand on his shoulder, I gently pull him closer.

"Hugs," I reply, wrapping him in my arms.

He tenses up for a moment, then relaxes into the hug, his arms going around me too. My shoulders drop and I lean into this warm, strong man, who has come to mean so much to me, so fast. There's something about him. It's just us. We are on the same wavelength.

"Are you ready for a drive?" I ask quietly in his ear.

He nods his head without saying anything.

"Perfect."

We let go and he starts to head round the car to the passenger door.

"Hold up." I run past him and grab the door handle. Opening the door for him, "For you sir."

"You didn't have to open my door, Ryder!" His face gets all red from blushing and I play it off as if I didn't notice.

"Don't worry about it. It makes me feel good," I say, smiling at him as he gets in.

Chapter Ten

Leo

WHAT IS HAPPENING RIGHT now?

We've been driving for a few minutes now, and neither of us has said anything, me staring out of the window, watching the silent world pass by us. I turn my head to look at Ryder, but when he turns his head to look back at me, I freak out and look away again quickly.

"You okay, Leo?" he asks, setting his hand on my forearm.

Giggling, "Yeah I'm okay, just wondering where we are going?"

Liar. Tell him how you wanted to kiss him after that amazing hug.

"Well, I'm still new here so maybe the local could throw out some ideas?"

"Oh right, that's me. Umm, I don't know any place at night since I don't go out much without Nina."

"Oh really? I'm honored to have you with me tonight then. I think I have an idea where to go. Here, pick a song to play for the ride." He hands me his phone and I look for the perfect song for the moment.

"Okay don't judge me, but I've had this one song stuck in my head after watching a movie a few nights ago."

"Should I be nervous?"

"No," I say, laughing.

I hit play on "Unwritten" and the song starts.

"Ohhhh. Okay, so we're playing hits, are we?"

"I guess we are!" I smile big and start singing along, letting myself feel the energy of the song and the moment. *"Staring at the blank page before you open up the dirty window!"* I sing as I roll down the window to feel the wind in my hair and skin.

I let the song take over my thoughts and sing with no care in the world. Ryder makes me feel safe and comfortable. I don't need to hide myself from him, I never did. At this moment, right now, I feel completely whole. With all these emotions running through me, I let my impulsive thoughts take over, unbuckling my seatbelt and lifting half my body out the window.

"Woah! Leo, what are you doing!" Ryder quickly has his arm around my body to hold me steady.

His touch on my body brings me back to the reality of what I was doing.

"Haha, I'm just enjoying the moment!" I say as I sit back down in the car.

I turn to look at Ryder and see him smiling as he stares at the road ahead and shakes his head.

"What?" I giggle.

"I love this side of you, Leo. I've never seen you look so free. What had me was how you just threw yourself out the window without warning."

"Oh," Did I show too much of myself? "My bad. I hope I didn't creep you out."

"Never. I loved it." He smiles.

I smile.

He smiles bigger.

Looking out the window, trying to see where Ryder is taking us, I notice we are near the main park in town.

"Are we going to the park?" I ask as he parks on the side of the road.

"I come here from time to time to find some peace, and I wanted to share some of that with you."

That's so sweet of him, but why this park?

"I wouldn't mind some peace right now actually."

"Perfect. Let's take a walk, there's a bridge I always go to nearby."

I nod as we get out of the car and start to walk towards the bridge.

As we get closer to the bridge, that I've always walked by growing up, I notice that it looks very different. There are more lights and, it seems, they have added a small waterfall nearby. I guess I haven't been here for a long time. It seems more peaceful than it once was. Ryder walks a little further than me but waits at the start of the bridge for me to catch up.

"Ready?" He looks at me with a smirk on his beautiful face.

"Ready for what?" I am so confused right now.

"Give it five seconds. Five. Four. Three. Two. One."

More lights turn on around the bridge and the waterfall, illuminating it in a magical light. I'm speechless as I turn to the railing.

"Woah, I—I didn't know they upgraded the bridge. How did you find out about this?"

"I just happened to be here after a long day to unwind and, right before I was about to leave, this happened. It made me feel so much better and now I come here all the time when I need to think or clear my head."

This is the moment I've always wanted with someone. Only one thing could make this better.

"Hey, Leo?" Ryder asks from behind me.

I turn from the view to look into Ryder's blue eyes, shining so beauti-fully in the lights.

"Mm-hmm" I whisper.

"Can I ask you something?" he says, ducking his gaze as he reaches out to fiddle with the cord of my hoodie. He seems nervous, which isn't like him.

"Anything. I'm an open book."

He takes a deep breath in and exhales, then, "Do you like me?"

What did he just ask me?

Do I like him?

What is happening?

This isn't happening, it has to be a dream.

"Because I like you. I like you so much." He says it in a rush, almost breathlessly, like he is letting all his worries go.

I take a step back, too confused to respond.

Ryder steps towards me, closing the gap between us.

"If you want me to stop, say stop Leo, because I'm sorry, I can't wait for an answer." He reaches with his hand, grabbing the back of my neck, and our lips lock together.

The world around me slips away with every touch of his tongue teasing at my lips. I let out a quiet moan. He turns my neck a little to deepen the kiss, making my body shiver with pleasure. Every cell in my body stands still with his lips on mine. Ryder softens the kiss and, as he pulls away, moans from the back of his throat. The sounds sends a jolt of electricity to my dick.

"I'm going to take that as a yes," he says softly, leaning his forehead on mine.

I look up into those blue eyes. "Yes," I whimper and I go in for another kiss, but this kiss is rougher. It's like we both need it. Crave it.

I kiss him as if my lungs were running out of oxygen, and his lips were my only way of getting it.

But then my brain starts whirling and I pull away.

"What is happening right now?"

"What do you mean?" he asks, as he tries to go in for another kiss.

"Why me? Why do you like me?" I pull my hand away from his face.

"Leo," he whispers. He reaches for my face and rubs my cheek with his thumb, slowly, giving me goosebumps.

"From the moment I saw those brown eyes, you had me head-over-heels. I'm so sorry I took this long to express how I've been feeling."

"I thought you were straight, honestly, and that Jenni was your girl-friend. I never thought you would like a guy like me."

"A guy like you? What do you mean?" his brow furrows in confusion.

"Have you seen how I look? I don't scream sexy at all."

"Please don't speak about yourself like that, Leo! You are one of the sexiest people that I've ever laid my eyes on. You take my breath away whenever you walk into any room."

"You think so?"

"Leo, it's not that I think so. I know so. Now shut up and kiss me again before I go crazy, baby."

"Mmm, say that again."

"Say what again?"

"Call me baby again. I love the way it rolls off your lips."

"Oh," he smirks, leans closer to my ear, and whispers "Give me those lips . . . *baby*."

I'm done for.

Chapter Eleven

Ryder

BEEP. BEEP. BEEP. BEEP.

I wake up to the sound of my alarm, and I lay in bed smiling. Last night felt like a dream. The only way I knew that it was real when I got home was the way my lips were still swollen from making out with Leo—all the way from the bridge to the car. I touch one fingertip to my lips, remembering. I still feel his lips on mine and I want them even more now. I didn't expect myself to tell him how I felt last night, but when we were there, in such a romantic spot, with all the lights hitting him perfectly, it just felt right and I went for it.

My phone dings with a text notification and I reach for it. The only name I want to see is on my phone screen: Leo's. I'm so glad we finally exchanged numbers last night before I dropped him off.

Leo: Good morning! I had a really great time last night.

Ryder: So did I! I'm excited to hang out later and talk about the booth.

Leo: Why wait?

Ryder: Someone's being confident ;)

Leo: Oh sorry! Was I being too forward?

Ryder: Not at all baby. I actually loved it, and I wouldn't mind seeing you now. I'll order us some food as well. So get your cute self to my house. I'll text you the address when you're ready. <3

Leo: Food! Give me twenty minutes!

As I reread our conversation, I feel butterflies in my stomach and I smile. I love seeing Leo come out of his shell, and I intend to explore him more.

"Oh shit!" I sit up in bed and look around my bedroom. *This place is a disaster.* I check my phone to see how long till Leo will get here. He said twenty minutes . . .

"Fuck!" I get out of bed, still in my boxers as I run around the entire apartment trying to make it look like a adult lives here.

I hear a soft knock on the door and I stop in my tracks.

"Who is it?" I ask, breathing heavily.

"It's Leo!"

I look around the apartment to see if I missed anything. It seems to look good enough for the time I had. I go to open the door, but I look down. I'm still in my boxers!

"Shit!" I whisper. "Coming!" I run to my bedroom and grab shorts and a shirt, trying to put them on as I stumble back to the front door. Trying to put my leg in my shorts, I fall hard.

"Ryder? Are you okay?" I hear from the other side of the door.

"Yeah! Sorry, I'm coming!" I get up as fast as I can and open the door. Leo is standing there, smiling softly, a dark curl falling across his forehead. He looks as casually put-together as ever, in jeans and a dark-blue polo shirt, a messenger bag over one shoulder.

"There you are. Thought you forgot about me." His smile broadens as he looks at what I am wearing, "Cute outfit by the way." And then he giggles.

I look down and my mouth drops with embarrassment. I didn't realize that I grabbed *this* shirt. The one my cousins gave me a couple of years ago, as a gag gift, that makes me look like I'm a woman in a bikini. I look back up at him and my face gets very hot. "Umm, it's laundry day."

He laughs, "Sure it is! So, are you going to invite me in?"

He looks up at me at me, and I get lost in those brown eyes.

"Ryder?"

I snap back to reality. "Huh? Oh, yeah! Come in!"

He comes in and I shut the door behind him.

"My house is your house so make yourself comfortable. Do you want anything to drink?" I ask, heading towards the kitchen.

"I'm good, but you promised food, so I'll take you up on that offer."

I laugh. "Alrighty what are you feeling? I can get it delivered."

"Pancakes!"

"You read my mind" We both smile at each other. "Let me change into something better."

"No! I think it's kinda cute. Keep it on!"

I walk up to him and lean in close, very aware our lips are just inches away from each other.

"Why exactly do you think it is cute?" I ask quietly, unable to tear my eyes away from his lips. He doesn't answer, staring up at me, and I go in for a soft kiss, one hand lifting to his cheek. His lips part under mine and I slide my hand to the back of his head, pulling gently on his hair to tilt his head and deepen the kiss.

Our tongues dance with each other, forwards, backwards, give and take and Leo moans. I pull away, biting down gently on his lip as I do so, and whisper, "Now, that right there was sexy."

He opens his eyes and we stare at one another, breathing heavily together.

"Let's . . . umm let's get started?" He says looking dazed from what just happened.

I laugh at his cute expression and grab his hand, rubbing it with my thumb. "Okay, cutie."

He blushes as I guide him to the couch.

We sit and get comfortable. "Let me order the food now so we don't have to wait too long. What kind of pancakes do you want?"

"I'm fine with anything. I eat anything, so you pick."

I want to say a dirty joke about eating something, but I don't think we are there just yet.

"Sounds good! Let's get some French toast and strawberry banana pancakes! Would you like that?"

"That sounds amazing if you don't mind sharing?"

"With you? Never, handsome." I'm grinning, loving this back and forward between us. Loving having Leo in my space. He just smiles softly, his smooth cheeks darkening with a blush as he ducks his head. I drag my eyes away from him to send in the order, then put my phone on the end table near me.

"Okay, let us get this idea session started. What do you have so far for the booth?"

Leo sucks in a deep breath, turning to me and clasping his hands in his lap. "Well, I want to do something new this year. I just don't know what to do, honestly. Every other store has done something outside the box, and I just feel like all the ideas I have aren't good enough."

I hate to see him looking so uncertain, his fingers working together, eyes tight with strain. Leo clearly doesn't see himself as the amazing businessman and person I see him as.

"Let's start from square one. Before we move forward, I need you to know that I think whatever you have is enough, or even better than other people's booths. Let's get that straight, okay?"

"Okay." He smiles.

I could get lost in that smile.

"Good. Now give me one of those good ideas you had."

"For a while now, I've wanted to have people get their favorite book quotes on any type of merch they want."

"I love that idea, Leo! All you would need is a press machine to do that on bags and shirts. I think I know someone who may have one we could borrow."

"Wait, really? That would be perfect! I could just kiss you right now!" He stops and his face gets even brighter red than before.

"Then do it," I say, smirking at him.

He looks stunned by my comment, not responding in any way other than to sit there staring, with his mouth slightly open.

"If you don't, then I will," I reach over, grabbing his waist, and drag his body on top of mine. He looks shocked by the way I make him straddle me.

"Ryder, I'm too heavy to be on top of you. Let me get off."

I hold him firmly in place, stopping him from moving any inch of his body off of me.

"Leo, stop that. You feel perfect exactly where you are right now. Now, back to that kiss."

He reaches for my cheek and as his fingers rub softly on my skin making it feel like it's on fire. Then he glides his thumb over my lips, making me wet them the moment his touch is gone, chasing the taste of his skin on mine.

"Your lips are so soft and sexy," he murmurs.

"Then kiss them. I can't wait any longer."

"Patience is key, love," he says softly, his eyes focused on my lips as his thumb strokes my jaw.

My heart jumps out of my chest.

"Did you just call me . . . ?"

He leans forward, getting close to my face.

"Love? Yeah, I just did." Then he brings our lips together. His lips are so soft as they move against, but this kiss isn't gentle. It's needy. Asking for more. And taking everything I give. I slide my hand to his ass, grabbing as much as I can with my hands and squeeze. Leo moans into my mouth and it makes me go feral. My hands are all over his body, from his thighs to his hair. I pull away from the kiss, moving his head a little to the side to get my lips on his skin. Moving down from his jawline, I start kissing his neck hard as he moans louder in my ear making my dick get harder.

Breathing heavily, he tells me, "Bite down."

Fuck. He is going to make me cum without even trying to.

I bite down where his neck meets his shoulder and Leo's entire body goes rigid, his thighs gripping my legs, sending fire all over my body. I tease him with another bite and then a soft kiss, before I lean back, breathing hard.

"My turn now," he says. His eyes burn with hunger for more and he grabs both my wrists and with one swift move he has both my arms above my head as he starts to kiss my neck.

"Fuck, baby, you're driving me crazy," I moan in his ear.

He slides his other hand up my shirt, his fingers trailing slowly over my abs, giving me goosebumps, and making me shudder all over from the pleasure of his touch.

"Seems like someone is excited," he says as he pulls away from my neck to look down at my thick cock bulging in my shorts, and then back up at me.

Something clicks the moment I saw his face when he looked up from my bulge. The look of needing something and craving more of it resonates in me. I crave more of Leo. His face. His body. Him.

Holding Leo's waist, I flip us over so his back is on the couch and I'm on top of his body. I take off my shirt with one hand, throwing it somewhere on the floor. Leo gasps the moment he sees my chest. He starts to outline my arms with his hands but stops before reaching my torso.

I lower myself and kiss him, more roughly now. He seems to love it when I show how much I want him—need him. I feel his arms around me as we grind against each other.

I want to feel his skin on mine.

"Take off your shirt, baby," I say between kisses.

"What?" He pulls away.

"Take this off" I reach down to the hem of his shirt, about to pull it off, until he blocks me with his hands. Gently shoving my shoulders, he makes it clear he wants me to move, so I quickly get off him, as Leo sits up on the couch, pulling his shirt into place and trying to straighten his hair at the same time.

"I've got to go. Umm, sorry—I just remembered I had to do something for my mom." He jumps up and starts to grab his things.

"Leo, are you okay? Did I do something wrong? You don't need to leave." I get up as he zips up his bag. He won't meet my gaze, his eyes bouncing around as if he might have left something, but he's barely been here any time at all.

"No, no. You're fine. I'm just going to head out, okay? Yeah, umm, bye." He heads to the front door, still not looking at me, and when he opens it, the delivery man is there holding our food.

"Excuse me." Leo says, rushing past him.

"What about the food?" I yell when I get to the hallway, only to see the elevator doors close.

"What did I do wrong?" I whisper to myself.

"2A?" the delivery man asks.

"Yeah, that's me."

"$21.43 is your total."

"Right." I head back into the apartment to get the money off the table. Still confused with what happened, I hand the money to the guy, taking the bag from him. "Keep the change."

"Thank you, sir! Have a good day!"

I shut the door and looked at the food meant to be shared.

What did I do wrong?

Chapter Twelve

Leo

It's been a few days since I saw Ryder at his apartment.

Everything was going so well and then I had to ruin it by freaking out and running out of there, as if my life depended on it. I got so in my head when things got heated on the couch. I wanted to keep going and let him do everything I was fantasizing about.

But the moment he reached under my shirt, I panicked.

I never let myself be open fully when it came to showing my body during sex. Ever since losing my virginity, I have always worn a shirt to cover my upper body. None of the men complained so I assumed they wanted me to keep it on. No man wants to look at my body when they are wanting to be pleasured. That has been engraved in my mind since I was sexually active.

"Fuck." I hit my head on the front counter at the bookstore feeling like an idiot.

"You good?" Neens asks.

Lifting my head slightly to get a view of her, I sigh, "No. I'm so stupid."

"What did you do, Leo? Can't be as bad as the time you were picking up your Mom's birthday cake and dropped it." she laughs. I groan and hit my head on the counter again in frustration.

"Way to remind me, Nina! I forgot about that, and now I feel even dumber than before," I sigh.

"What happened?"

I take a deep breath, preparing myself for all the questions that are about to be asked. I haven't told her about what happened with Ryder. I wasn't ready yet, but it's Neens and I need to talk about it with someone. I lift my head to look at her and take a deep breath.

"Ryder kissed me."

"Shut the fuck up!" she screams, jumping up and down, "Where did it happen? How did it happen? Is he a good kisser? Wait, did you kiss him back? Dude, answer me!"

"Shhhhhhh!" I look around to make sure no one is paying attention to Neens freaking out. "Relax before someone hears you. I don't need this to get out before I can talk to him."

"Okay, okay. Now tell me what happened," she demands, leaning on the counter in front of me and gazing at me with eyes wide.

"The night that you ditched me for that stupid date, Ryder messaged me on Instagram. I told him how our parents were already drunk, and that I was bored. He asked me if I wanted to go for a drive, and I said yes."

"You're telling me you wouldn't have gone on this drive if it weren't for my date. So . . . technically this was all my doing?"

I roll my eyes at her, "Shut up and listen to the story because there is more."

She waves her hand motioning for me to keep going.

"He asked me where we should go since I'm the local, but I didn't know what to say so he picked. He ended up taking us to the park."

"The park? Why there?"

"Honestly, I was confused as well when we got there," I admit. "He took me to that old bridge near the center of the park, but it's been renovated with lights and a waterfall. It's . . . pretty. Relaxing. He told me that the bridge is his escape when he needs to calm his mind."

"Well, what happened?" Neens looks at me expectantly, arching brows rising.

"He—he asked me if I liked him."

Neens jaw shoots to the floor, "He did *not* ask you that?!"

"Mm-hmm, he did."

"Okayyy . . . and—?"

"I couldn't answer him. I could barely believe what was happening." I cringe, remembering how incapable of answering I had been. "But he didn't wait for my answer and he—he kissed me," I say in a tone full of wonder, thinking about how Ryder pulled me into him and the way it sent goosebumps all over my body.

I reach up to my lips to touch them, remembering how his soft lips felt on mine.

He kissed me.

He *kissed me.*

He kissed me.

Lost in my thoughts of the kiss, Neens snaps me back into reality. "Earth to Leo!! Was the kiss good?"

"Yes. Breathtaking." I press my hands to my heated cheeks. "I didn't know what to do . . . so I kissed him harder."

"Woah, this is a new side of you, Leo. I'm loving it!" Neens straightens, grinning widely at me. "I'm happy for you!"

"Yeah, well, I was happy," I say and sigh. "Until I fucked it all up a couple of days ago."

"What do you mean, you fucked it up?"

"Ryder offered to go over booth ideas with me. He asked me to come over to his place and I was overthinking how I was going to be alone with him in his apartment."

"You went to his house? Alone!?" Neens is now standing with both hands on her hips, looking like some beauty pageant drill sergeant.

"I'm not a child Neens and stop fucking yelling!"

She calms herself down enough to be quiet and waits for more.

"So, I got there, and things were going great. We came up with the idea for the booth and ordered some food. Then things got a little more heated when I said I should kiss him for helping me . . . he told me to kiss him and I went for it. Then—" I lean on the counter again and Neens copies me, before I continue, in a voice barely above a whisper, "then he moved me onto his lap and, honestly, I started to get into it. The next thing I knew, I was spread out on the couch with him on top of me."

"You were what!" Neens covers her mouth in shock.

"He kissed me with so much passion that I got lost in the high. But then he reached inside my shirt and my mind went from wanting more to feeling disgusting," I tell her with a sigh.

"Oh, Leo," she sighs.

"I know. You can stop looking at me like that. I know!" I say as I push back the chair and get up to leave. I can't handle seeing the disappointed look in her eyes.

Chapter Thirteen

Ryder

I've been in a funk for over a week, since that morning Leo fled from my apartment. Things have been awkward, and we've only texted about the booth. It's like that night at the bridge and the morning at my house never happened. Which is fucking up my head.

Did I do something wrong?

I need to know because I can't stop thinking about his soft lips on mine. The way his body felt as he sat on my lap. I loved the feeling of his body grounding me to the moment of just me and him. I need to know what is happening between us.

"Are you excited for the block party? It seems like people are starting to set up their booths already. Shouldn't you be doing the same with Leo?" Jenni questions me from the store window making me come back to the reality of what today was.

It's the day of the block party and, after only texting about the booth, this will be the first time seeing Leo or even having a full conversation with him. I don't have anxiety issues normally, but today I know how it truly feels.

"Mm-hmm, I'm about to head over to our booth to start setting up. Are you sure you can handle the store on your own today? It's going to be packed. If you need me to—"

"Ryder, get the hell out there. The staff and I got this," she orders me, with so much attitude that I get up and leave with nothing but my phone.

I'm glad I have Jenni around to get me out of my head, but it doesn't last long. As I walk out of the coffee shop, it's strange to see people walking on the road, but they closed Maple Drive for the party. Leo's booth is set up in front of the bookstore.

"Well, hello, young man!" I hear from behind me. Turning around, I see Leo's mom and dad carrying boxes to the booth.

"Hello, Mr. and Mrs. Blanco! It's so nice to see you both again. Do you need help with those boxes?"

"Oh, that would be lovely Ryder.."

"Sounds good!" I grab the boxes from them and head into the booth, setting them on the table with a loud thud.

"What the fuck!" Leo snaps, popping up from under the table, "You scared the shit out—" Leo freezes, "Oh, Ryder, I didn't know it was you."

Why does he sound so disappointed?

"Sorry, I didn't mean to scare you. I was helping your parents with boxes," I say cautiously, the tension in the air palpable. I clear my throat, looking about me "What should we set up first?"

I have to talk to him. This doesn't feel right. I can't bear that we've gone from whatever was developing between us to Leo being disappointed I've turned up at all.

"My dad was nice enough to set up the shirt press for us, so we don't have to worry about that part, and he taught me how to use it!" Leo smiles at me, helping me breathe a little easier.

"Good! I'm glad you got things set up. Are all these boxes the blank merch things?"

"Yeah, they are blank tote bags in various colors so we can press on people's favorite book quotes." Leo opens the top box, showing me the folded tote bags inside. "Did you bring those coupons for the coffee shop we talked about?"

"Yes, I did!" I reach into my pocket thankful that I made cards for the booth. I hand them to Leo and our fingers touch for a moment, sending heat tingling up my arm.

"Thanks, Ryder," Leo says, his voice cracking like he is struggling to hold back emotion,

I can't take this confusion anymore and blurt out, "Leo, can we talk about what happened?"

My heart beats faster with every second I wait for his answer. Leo looks at me with his beautiful brown eyes—*oh how I've missed gazing into those eyes*—and then sighs.

"Ryder, let's talk after the block party is done, is that okay?" he asks, wincing.

"Yeah, that's perfect. Let's get this block party started." I give him a big smile, trying to make things more comfortable for both of us, even though I was buzzing uncomfortably inside at the thought something is wrong.

"Let's do it!"

"Here is your tote, ma'am! Thank you so much for your support!" Leo says to our final customer.

"Yes, thank you. I put a coupon in the tote for the coffee shop as well! Please visit whenever you can!" I tell the customer as she walks away.

I turn to Leo as soon as the customer is out of sight.

"I'm sorry we didn't win this year, but runner up isn't too bad right?" I tell him, trying to make him feel a little better. Leo turns to me, finally giving me the attention I've been needing.

"It's okay. Winning really didn't matter to me much. What really mattered was the person who was with me," he says blushing.

"Can we talk now?" I ask, shifting closer to him, but then a shout comes from the dissipating crowds.

"Boys!" We turn and see Nina walking towards our tent.

I take a deep breath in and exhale, letting go of my frustration.

"Hey Neens!" Leo greets her. "I thought you weren't coming till later for dinner?"

"Nah, my date got canceled so I came earlier," she says, hugging Leo. "Hello, Ryder!" She giggles at me and Leo elbow bumps her.

Did he tell her what happened?

"So, you had the day off for no reason then?" Leo says, giving her a look.

Nina side-eyes Leo before redirecting her attention back to me, making me laugh.

"Hey Nina, how have you been? Sorry about your date."

"It's all good. I wasn't really into her that much. I just wanted someone to buy me food."

Leo starts to laugh at the comment.

"Neens, that's so fucking you!" Leo says with sass. I've missed seeing that relaxed sass. He's been tightly wound around me ever since I got here.

"What?! I wanted a burger and she offered. Now I'm starving and cranky. Leo, let's go before I make a scene. And you know I will. I'm not pretty when I'm hangry."

My eyebrows shoot up and my eyes widen, this girl is quite the character.

"Looks like she needs to be fed, Leo. You guys go ahead, I can finish cleaning the booth."

"You sure Ryder? I can help out before leaving, it's not a problem."

"I'm sure, but do me a favor?"

"Yeah, what is it?" He looks at me with his beautiful brown eyes. I want to look at them every day.

"Answer my phone call later?"

Leo looks at me nervously as if his first instinct is to refuse, but then he takes a deep breath, closing his eyes for a moment. "I will," he says and smiles, making my heart melt and my body finally relaxes for the first time today.

Chapter Fourteen

Leo

AFTER HAVING DINNER WITH Neens, we went back to my house to play games with my parents. Things got a little too intense for my liking, so I jumped out of the game to start getting ready for bed. I'm in the bathroom when I hear a knock on my bathroom door over the sound of the shower running.

"Hey, Leo! I'm heading out for the night. I'll see you tomorrow at work," Neens yells.

"Dude, I hear you just fine, you don't need to yell. I'll see you tomorrow. Love you!"

"Love you more! Bye!"

I shake my head at her antics, then turn to the basin. I stare at my half naked body in the mirror, judging every imperfection I see.

Why would someone like Ryder want to touch me?

I'm nervous enough about this phone call. I can't think like this. This mindset won't help me achieve anything. Talking to him calms every nerve in my body. His voice grounds my very core to this earth. So why can't I fully let myself be free with him? I can't push him away like I do to all those who try to get me to understand who I am or who I could be.

I go through the dresser, grabbing a pair of comfy shorts and a white t-shirt, before air drying on my bed as I check my phone. No missed texts or calls from Ryder.

"When is he going to call me?" I sigh.

What is it about him that gets me so wound up? I know how to handle myself. Why not with him?

I set my phone down on the bed and reach for the shorts. A text tone alerts me and I rush to grab my phone, my shorts halfway on, tripping over myself and falling to the ground with a big thud.

"Leo! Estas bien?" I hear my mom yell from the living room.

"Si! Sorry!" I yell back.

I push myself off the floor and quickly pull on my shorts properly. I grab my phone, clicking on the button to turn it on.

"Finally!" I see a text from Ryder and as I'm about to click on it, my phone pops up with Ryder's name on the screen.

"Shit! Fuck! Act normal!" I scramble to get comfy on my bed, before taking a deep breath in and sliding the arrow on my vibrating phone to accept the call.

"Hello?" I whisper.

"Hey, Leo."

An awkward silence takes over the call.

I bite the bullet.

"Ryder, I'm so sorry for how I've been treating you. I know it seems like I didn't like what was happening, but trust me I did like it. I wanted more of it and —"

"Then why did you leave?" Ryder interrupts. "Did I do something wrong?"

"No, Ryder, you didn't do anything wrong at all. The truth is . . ." I hesitate for a moment.

"Baby, you can trust me."

The way he says *baby* sends chills down my spine and gives me the courage to be vulnerable.

"It's my body."

"What do you mean? Your body is perfect the way it is."

"I don't believe that Ryder," I reply, the words spilling out of me, quicker, and quicker. "I can't trust someone saying that to me. I'm fat, and I know it. No one wants to see me naked. I don't even want to see myself naked. Why would you want someone fat and ugly?"

I close my eyes, fighting the urge to throw my phone away from me, to run from this conversation.

I can do this . . . I think.

"Baby," he whispers. "I hate to hear you think like this. You can't assume what I'm into and who I'm into is *you*. How your body feels on top of mine ignites a flame that can't be extinguished until your skin is on mine. Even then my body is an inferno of greed. I want you to be all mine, no one else's. I wish you could see yourself the way I see you."

I breathe heavily, letting his words sink in. He sounds genuine. And that hint of possessiveness is possibly the hottest thing I have ever heard. *Can I trust him? Could I do this with him without panicking?* Remembering the way his cock felt when I was on top of him, I feel my cock pulse.

"Ryder . . . I want you more than you know. When you look at me with those blue eyes I can't help myself. I—I wanted to keep going—I didn't mean to run. I've been like this for so long that I don't realize how much

I let myself down. Trust me, what you feel, I feel ten times more. I wanted my lips all over you. But I freaked out, and I'm sorry."

"Don't be sorry baby," he says quickly, then continues more softly, "I appreciate you being open about this. I know it's not easy to be vulnerable about your body. I hope you can see that I like your body the way it is. I'm someone who gets to know the person before I get physical, and with you, I want it all."

I can't believe this man is in my life. How is it possible that someone so beautiful is so considerate as well? And wants *me*.

No wonder I'm falling for him.

Oh . . . wow.

I'm falling for him, and I can't stop it. I smile as the sense of how amazing that is spreads through my body. This man makes me feel like maybe I can be brave.

"I want you, Ryder, I do," I say.

"I want you so much, Leo." Ryder's voice is even deeper than usual, and I hear him suck in a breath. "I can't stop thinking about being on top of you, half naked with my cock hard, wanting you to touch it."

"Fuck, Ryder . . ." I whimper, as heat rushes to my groin, my cock plumping.

"The way you had me going crazy with lust. I can't stop thinking about it."

Are we about to have phone sex?

I vote yes.

"I've never done this before," I admit, feeling the redness on my face as I think about my lack of experience.

"Done what?"

"This. Phone sex," I say in a soft voice.

Ryder chuckles and the sound sends a bolt of electricity from the top of my spine to the tip of my shaft, making it stiffen more.

"Only if you want to?"

"I want to so badly, Ryder."

"Good, because I want your lips all over me. Shall I tell you exactly where?"

I whimper. No other word for it. "Please," I beg.

My cock is hard, tenting my shorts as I shift to get comfortable on my pillows. It's taking so much of me not to get up and run to him. However, phone sex will do the trick for right now.

"First, I want those soft lips kissing mine, claiming me," Ryder says over the phone, his voice deep and slow. "Second, I want your fingers to trace every inch of my body, until they hit the one growing spot that wants to be touched by you."

Fuck.

Just hearing that almost makes me cum in my shorts. Clutching my phone tightly to my ear, I reach down with the other hand and press my dick through my shorts.

"Then, I'll make you use that glorious tongue to lick me from the base of my cock to the wet tip. It's oozing with precum, baby, all because of you."

Oh, shit . . . I need to be touched. No, I need Ryder's cock in my mouth, that's what I need.

"Fuck, love, I want that so bad right now," I mutter, biting my bottom lip at the idea of having his cock near me.

"Leo, I'm so hard right now. I need to cum. Are you hard?"

I whimper, pressing down harder on my cock. "Ryder . . . I don't think I can get any harder."

"Pull your dick out and stroke it for me, baby. I want to hear you moan."

Boy, was I wrong about getting harder. He knows what he is doing.

I freeze for a moment, not knowing what to say to this man who knows all the right words to drive me wild, but the insistent throbbing of my cock in my shorts has me doing what he asks. Shoving my shorts down just far enough that my cock pops out, slapping against my soft abdomen, leaving sticky precum on my skin.

"I'm so wet Ryder. I'm going to cum quick if I start to jerk off," I confess, fingers gripping the sheet as I try to resist touching myself.

"Mmmm, baby, I'm glad I make you wet as you make me. I don't care if you cum quickly, I want you to feel good."

I grab my shaft and slide my hand up and down, a rush of pleasure filling my cock and spreading through me as I think of Ryder's hands all over me. "Fuck, this feels so good, love."

"Good boy, I want you to feel good." Oh wow, why does that make me feel so *much?* "Keep going," Ryder continues, "I want to hear you moan. I'm right there with you. My cock is hard as fuck wanting your touch." He breaks off and I hear him panting into the phone.

"Are you . . . ? Oh god, you *are*," I whisper into my phone.

"Touching myself? Yes," he says harshly, panting louder.

Knowing he is touching his thick cock with his hands is making me feral. I've never felt like this before, but something is taking me over the edge.

"Ryder . . ." I moan, stroking myself tighter, faster. "I'm close . . . ngh," I grunt in a deep voice.

"Damn, hearing you moan for me is driving me crazy, Leo. I'm almost there too. Cum with me."

I can't take it. I need to let this load out.

Then, "Leo, can you call me something?"

"Mmm, what is it?"

"Can you call me Daddy?"

Fuck me . . . with that deep voice and the word Daddy, he pushes me over the edge. "Mmm . . . Fuck . . . yesss . . . Daddy . . ." I grunt as my cum shoots out of my cock, hitting my shirt.

"Shit Leo, that's so fucking sexy. Fuck! I'm cumming, baby, I—" I hear Ryder moan loudly with pleasure and then low grumbles as he calms down from the high of his orgasm.

I wipe my hand on my messed up shirt, but we both stay quiet for a bit, just breathing heavily on the phone. I'm enjoying each and every sound we make. That was one of the best orgasms I've ever felt and that was just phone sex. I can't wait to see what real sex is like with Ryder.

"That was . . ." I try.

I don't even have words for what just happened.

"Sexy as fuck?"

"Yeah, that," I say, and we laugh together.

"Leo?"

"Yes?"

"Are we okay?" Ryder's voice has lost the deep confidence he brought to phone sex. He sounds unsure. Worried.

"We are perfect," I reassure him. I can hear the relief in his answering sigh, and it brings me joy that I can give him that peace of mind. "I'm sorry again for how I treated you, Ryder. I was just scared."

"Leo . . . You don't need to say sorry to me. I'm here for you always. I—" Ryder breaks off, takes an audible breath in, then continues, "I don't do this with just anyone. You mean a lot to me."

A broad smile stretches my face. What did I do to deserve this? This man makes me feel more wanted than I ever have in the past, more content than I have been in maybe years.

"You mean a lot to me as well Ryder. I've never done this with anyone. I'm glad you were my first." Then I yawn, loudly.

"You sleepy, baby?" Ryder asks.

I grab some tissues to clean up, throwing them in the direction of my wastebasket, not caring to clean up more. "Mm-hmm, after that I'm very relaxed. I'm glad we talked."

"And had phone sex?" I can hear the smirk in his voice as I pull my blanket over me.

I giggle softly, "Yes, especially that."

I snuggle into my pillow and put my phone next to my head. "Ryder?"

"Yes, baby?"

"Fall asleep with me?"

"On one condition, you try to stop putting yourself down. If you keep talking badly about the man I care about, I'll have to kick your ass."

We both chuckle. "It's a deal," I say, smiling softly.

"Good. Sleep well, handsome" he whispers.

"You too."

Chapter Fifteen

Ryder

I WAKE TO THE sound of birds chirping and sunshine that's bright even behind my closed eyelids. Sleepily rolling over, I open my eyes and see my phone on the pillow next to me, still connected to the call with Leo. In the quiet of my apartment, I can hear him softly breathing and it makes my heart flutter. Last night was amazing and if that was a hint of being sexual with Leo then I'm ready for more. I lie in bed listening to Leo breathe, wishing he was with me. Staring at my phone, I allow myself a minute to imagine a future with this wonderful man, excited for what Leo and I can be.

Not wanting to wake Leo up, I whisper, "I'm falling in love with you, Leo, and I can't wait to tell you one day."

I end the call but send Leo a quick good-morning text letting him know I was leaving for work soon. Syncing up the speaker for my shower, I set the phone down, rolling out of bed to get ready for this beautiful day as my 'Good Mood' playlist blasts from the bathroom.

"Good morning, Mrs. Johnson! How are you doing this beautiful morning?"

"Well, hello, young man! I'm doing quite well! Always glad to come to The Crush."

I chuckle, glad that the locals found a nickname for the shop. Honestly, I'm just happy that we have regulars now. "We are happy to have you! Are you having your usual today? Maybe a muffin as well?"

"You know me so well, don't you Ryder?"

"Yes, I do! It's always nice to have you here." The Johnsons have been so kind to me since meeting them, and now they're part of the coffee-shop family we're growing. Not having my own family here has been hard, but moving here has been the best thing for me. It led me to Leo, after all, and he is all I need.

I ring up Mrs. Johnson on the tablet checkout and move to the espresso machine. The doorbell rings and I lift my head to greet the new arrival,

"Good morning, welcome to—" I pause, seeing Leo walk in. The man who called me "Daddy" during phone sex. My mood instantly gets ten times better. *Play it cool, Ryder.* "Hey," I nod casually with a smirk.

"Hey, Ryder," Leo flashes his adorable smile at me, and all I want to do is take him to the back office and lick every inch of him from his neck down his torso. I want him all to myself, like I said during our phone call. Leo belongs to me, and I want the whole world to know it.

I hear someone cough and it brings me out of my fantasy about Leo and his body. *Right. At work.*

"Are you going to introduce me to your friend, young man?" Mrs. Johnson asks with a small smile, eyes twinkling at me like she knows all my secrets.

"Oh! I apologize, Mrs. Johnson," I say, feeling the heat of a blush in my cheeks and wishing I could play it cooler. "This is Leo: the owner of the bookstore across the street." Only then do I look behind Leo, not having realized that Nina has been here the entire time.

"And I'm his amazing best friend, Nina, who also works at the bookstore," Nina says as she waves at Mrs. Johnson and then shoots me a stink eye.

Rubbing the back of my neck awkwardly, I blurt, "Yes! Nina as well! Sorry I didn't see you at first."

"You're fine. I know your mind is elsewhere," she says, winking at me and I blush again.

"Neens, cut it out!" Leo exclaims as he elbows her, but she just laughs. Turning his back on Nina, Leo gives a little wave to Mrs. Johnson. "Hello, Mrs. Johnson. I've heard amazing things about you from my parents! They love seeing you around the town. Sorry we haven't met before."

"Don't worry, love," Mrs. Johnson replies, patting him on the arm. "You kids are always running around, keeping busy. It's always a pleasure to meet young folk who brighten up my day, like our handsome coffee shop owner here."

"You're the beautiful one here Mrs. Johnson! Just don't tell your husband I said that," I say with a grin and we all laugh, but then the older lady turns back to me.

"My granddaughter is coming to town soon, Ryder. You would just love her! Maybe you can show her around when she's here?"

There's a moment of silence as I turn my head to look at Leo, trying to find a way to answer the question without mentioning anything we haven't yet discussed. Nina coughs to get our attention, making both Leo and I blush as I realize I've been standing staring at him instead of answering the question.

I look back to Mrs. Johnson. "I would love to, but right now I'm very busy with the coffee shop. Bring her on by to get a cup of coffee and muffin on me," I say, and she smiles at me. *Phew, explanation dodged!* "Oh . . . let me get your order." I rush to the bar and get her things ready. As I prepare the drink order, I get glimpses of them and I see how comfortable Leo is with people. He shines confidence in front of others, but he doesn't see it. I want to help him to find that side of him that is already there. He needs to know he is worthy of love, and I want to be the man that gives it to him.

I return with the order in hand, "Here is your order, Mrs. Johnson. I added an extra muffin for your husband as well."

"You didn't have to Ryder."

"I wanted to." I smile at her and she reaches over the counter for a hug. When she lets go, my gaze goes to Leo again. From the corner of my eye, I can see Mrs. Johnson looking at me

She leans in again to whispers in my ear, "I like him. Treat him well, he's a keeper."

Hugging me, she makes her approval of Leo and me clear. I didn't know how much I needed someone to say that to me, until I realized how good it made me feel.

"Now I should head back to my husband. He must be wondering where I've gone. You kids have a great day, you hear?"

"Thank you for coming in Mrs. Johnson, it's always a pleasure," I say.

She gives Nina, then Leo, a hug, whispering something in his ear, before walking to the door, coffee cup in hand.

I wonder what she said to him?

As the door closes, I refocus. "What brings you guys to the shop? Other than getting drinks, I assume," I ask Leo and Nina.

"We just finished our shift at the store and I wanted my caffeine fix before going to the gym. Of course, Leo wanted to come for other reasons. Aren't I right, Leo?" she teases. Leo pales and Nina laughs hysterically.

"Nina!" he barks in a low voice that I wish he would use with me.

I start laughing along with Nina, and a blush brings life back to Leo's face.

I find Leo's eyes. "I'm grateful for the other reason," I smirk at him. "Nina, go order your drink and let them know it's on the house," I say to her wanting to have some alone time with Leo.

"You sure? Wait no, I'm going before you change your mind!" She quickly joins the line that formed while we were talking.

Leo shakes his head at his best friend, "Sorry about her, she can be a lot, I hope you don't mind that I have talked to her a little about us. I mean . . . ah . . . yeah, what has happened," he says, blushing as he stumbles over his words.

I laugh at how adorable Leo is when he's trying not to freak out. "Don't worry about it," I say reassuringly, "I kinda figured when she was giving those little hints. I'm glad you told someone. I'm not going to hide how I feel about you."

Leo smiles, "Should we sit or do you need to get back to work?"

I look back at the bar, where Jenni is now helping customers. "Hey, Jenni, I'm going to take my lunch. Is that cool?"

Jenni looks up from the checkout and nods at me, letting me know it's fine.

"Thanks!" I turn back to Leo, lifting the bar-flap to join him on the other side of the counter. "Want to sit outside? It's a nice day out."

"Sounds perfect! Lead the way."

Walking out to the tables, we find one in the shade. I can't stop taking mental pictures of Leo. He looks so good in any light. The way the sun makes his tan skin look so lickable . . . hot lust spreads all over my body with the thought of ripping his clothes off.

"So, about our phone call . . ." Leo's eyes have a fire in them, igniting my flame even more, as he finds my gaze.

"Leo, that call was everything and more," I say quickly. "I hope I didn't push you too far."

"No! I just wanted to say that I enjoyed it . . . a lot. Like, *a lot.*"

We both blush at the memory of moaning in each other's ears. Wanting to do anything to get more of that beautiful color in his cheeks, I lean in closer and, in a deep whisper, I say, "Wait until we do it in person, baby," and then wink.

Leo bites his bottom lip, and the sight sends a jolt of electricity to my cock. I shift in my seat, but I can see Leo practically melting out of his chair. Getting even closer to him, I use my tongue to outline his ear.

"Mmm, baby . . . Daddy loves to turn you on." I moan, wanting to make Leo squirm. He lets out a small whimper, but then the sound of a chair scraping on concrete makes us jump apart, bringing us back to reality.

"Did I interrupt something?" Nina's eyebrows flash upward as she sets down her drink.

I lean back on my chair, keeping my eyes on Leo and making sure my groin is under the table. "Absolutely nothing," I say with a wink at Leo, giving him a smirk. Leo avoids eye contact with both of us, leaning forward on the table in a way that makes me hope he's hiding the same problem as me.

"Okayyyy . . . well, I guess we can talk about Leo's birthday then!" Nina cheers, looking from me to Leo and back again. Leo's eyes go wide and he waves a hand frantically at Nina, shushing her. She looks confused, asking, "What?! Was he not supposed to know?"

I look at Leo, confused myself as to why he would want to hide that from me, and, I realize, more than a little hurt.

Leo looks at both Nina and me, "No, no, I just wanted to tell him myself, I guess. And I haven't."

"My bad! Sorry I didn't think about that," Nina says with a small smile.

"It's all good," he assures her, then turns to me. "So—uh—we are having a birthday dinner with my parents, and I wanted to extend an invitation to you."

My heart jumps with joy, knowing he wants me to be a part of a special day with his family, and a wide smile spreads across my face.

"I would be honored, Leo. When is the big day?"

"It's next week," he says happily.

"Thank you for inviting me. I'm excited to celebrate with everyone!"

"Of course!" Leo gives me a bashful smile but holds my gaze. I nearly reach for his hand, but Nina interrupts the moment.

"Ryder, have you heard about the town's annual masquerade ball?"

"I have not!" I say, turning to her. "I've been busy with the store and other things . . . I haven't been checking up on town events." My eyes find Leo's again, and I give him a wink, meaning to let him know that he is my "other things".

"Well, it's the same week as Leo's birthday and I've been trying to get him to go for years. He never goes with me, maybe this year could be different." Nina grabs Leo's arm and squeezes it.

"Maybe." I smile, keeping my eyes locked on Leo, but he drops his gaze and pushes his chair back.

"I think it's time for us to go, Neens. You've got to hit the gym and I—umm—have to go do something for my Mom," Leo says, scratching his head and looking all kinds of awkward.

I chuckle, knowing that is his way of trying to avoid something.

"It was nice to see you, Ryder!" Nina waves as she walks away, "I'll get you a flier with all the deets on the Ball."

I get up quickly to grab Leo by the hand before he follows her, "Wait, Leo. Can I ask you something?"

Leo's eyes focus on where our hands are holding and then his gaze lifts up my arms to my eyes.

"Umm . . . Yeah. What's up, Ryder?"

I clear my suddenly dry throat. "About your birthday—"

"Yeah?"

"Before your dinner, would you want to go out with me? Like on a date?" I can't believe how nervous I am, but even after everything, I'm not sure how Leo will respond. He freezes for a moment and I can feel his hand clench in mine.

"A date?"

"Mm-hmm. I would love to take you out for your birthday."

He takes a deep breath, releases it on a sigh, his hand relaxing in mine, then finally answers, "I would love that."

"Good" I huff, chuckling in relief, "because I wouldn't have taken no for an answer." He laughs, and the thought flashes across my mind that I need more of that warm laugh. "I'm going to make sure this is the best birthday you've ever had," I say, pulling him in for a hug.

Leo relaxes into the hug, "I know you won't let me down."

I pull away slightly, stare at this handsome man in my arms and let my impulses take over. I lean in and kiss him softly, but slowly on the cheek. His face gets red hot and I feel the heat on my lips. I pull away and his eyes dart around, looking around to see if anyone was watching. Why is he afraid of people seeing us? I have nothing to hide. He shouldn't either.

"Don't worry, baby, no one saw us. I want people to know you're mine. Don't you want people to know I'm yours?" I ask with a wink, and he smirks back at me but doesn't answer, so I let it go. "Go catch up with Nina before she kills me for keeping you from her."

Chapter Sixteen

Leo

A DATE?

With Ryder of all people. I can't believe that this is happening right now. I feel like I'm in a dream that is about to crash and burn. Everything good that happens to me always goes wrong. What if I fuck up this date, and he gets disgusted by me?

"I can't do this. This is too much," I grunt out as I sit on the couch in my living room.

"Dude, what's up with you? You have been acting weird lately." Neens flops right next to me with a bowl of ice cream.

"Ryder asked me out on a date," I admit.

Neens chokes on her ice cream and freaks out, shrieking, "AND WHEN WERE YOU GOING TO TELL ME THIS?!"

"He asked me the day we went to visit him after work," I say, finally looking Neens in the eyes.

"*Leo!* That was *three days ago*! What took you so long to tell me about this?" Neens raises an eyebrow in my direction as she sticks a spoonful of ice cream in her mouth.

"I don't know, okay? I wanted time to figure out my feelings before others added their thoughts." I sigh, breathing out the pressure of keeping this in.

"I thought you wanted this, Leo?" Neens asks, laying her hand on my thigh, "You seem so happy when you talk about him or even think about him."

"I do want this, but I get in my head about everything. What if I fuck something up and he truly sees me for who I am?"

"And . . . who are you?" Her body language is tense waiting for my response.

"I'm not good enough for him, and when he finally realizes it, I'll be heartbroken." I look away from Neens, knowing she will give me a death stare for talking bad about myself.

"Leo, your feelings are valid."

Wait what? I turn to face her, and she has sadness in her eyes that I've never seen before.

"I know how you're feeling because I felt the same way in my last relationship."

I'm shocked to hear this from her, she is always in relationships. "Wait, but you go on dates. You seem happy about it, and I'll be honest I've been envious of you."

"You've never asked *why* I always go on these dates, have you?"

"I assumed you had all these options of people, so I never questioned anything."

"I've always kept my dating life private to a certain extent with you, Leo. I'm not trying to hide anything, but whenever the topic of dating comes up you always have this negative mindset. It's hard to talk about that with you."

Have I been a shitty friend?

"I didn't realize . . . I'm so sorry Nina," I blurt out, my eyes on the floor, my cheeks hot. "I feel so terrible that I made everything about me, and never asked how you feel. I promise to change that."

"You don't need to apologize," Neens assures me, nudging my side gently. "I understand why you feel the way you do, that's why I stand by you. Everyone, even me, has insecurities and fears when it comes to dating. We all have things we don't like about ourselves, but we have to accept that what we hate about ourselves, other people don't see."

I grab her hands, turning towards her on the couch, my eyes fixed on her face. "Nina Katherine Rose. You are the best person and the best love I've ever had in my life. You and I were meant to be friends from the day we met as babies. You deserved better from me and from now on you should always be open with me about how you feel. You are worthy of love. I know this because being loved by you is the best feeling." My eyes start to water as I keep my gaze on Neens.

Neens also starts to tear up, saying huskily, "Te amo, Leo," as she leans in to hug me.

"Te amo," I let out as we hold each other.

"Now let's get you ready for this date tomorrow."

I nod and smile.

My alarm goes off for about five minutes before I turn it off. I stare at the ceiling thinking about what today will be like. My date with Ryder is in an hour, and I still haven't gotten up. I'm frozen from anxiety. I don't know how to get out of this. My bedroom door opens and Neens walks in, bouncing with every step.

"LEO, IT'S TIME TO GET UP!" She jumps on the bed, making it rock up and down, hitting me with my pillows.

"Okay! Damn! I'm getting up now. Calm yourself," I laugh. I'm glad Neens agreed to help me get ready. I get up and head to the bathroom to shower. "Pick my outfit?"

"Don't need to ask me twice!" After our talk last night, things between us will change. I need to learn to accept love from Ryder.

"Perfect! I won't take long." As I enter the bathroom, I find myself staring at all the imperfections that make me feel powerless. "You won't win today," I tell my insecure thoughts in the mirror. "Today is a good day. I am confident. I am loved."

I pee and shower, resolutely pushing away any negative thoughts about my body. I've just finished brushing my teeth when Neens yells from my room, "Leo! Hurry, you need to get dressed!"

I roll my eyes, tightening the towel around my waist as I walk back into my bedroom. "I'm here. Relax girly!" My eyes float to an outfit on my bed—a lavender shirt paired with black men's joggers, with some silver jewelry next to it. "Wait, these aren't my clothes." I look at Neens, confused.

She has a soft smile on her face. "Yup, I got you a new outfit for today."

"Neens, you didn't have to do that! Return them. I can find an outfit in my closet."

"Your style needed an update."

"Neens!"

"You know I'm right," she says, glaring at me with her hands on her hips. "You wear the same clothes every day just in different colors. You're going on an important date, so I made your decision."

She's right about my clothes. I guess it's time to accept the change. I stare at the outfit again, thinking about how it will look and feel on me.

"Honestly, I kinda like it. The jewelry ties it all together. Thank you Neens, this means a lot."

"Happy birthday, Leo." She leans in to hug me, and I hug her back. "Now go change, you need to leave soon."

"Neens, you're in my room . . ."

"Oh right! I'll give you a minute." She heads to the living room, shutting the door behind her.

I put on the new outfit and head to the living room where my mom and Neens are waiting for me. When they have me in their sights, they stop talking and both stare at me. I stop, gnawing on my lower lip as I shift anxiously from foot to foot.

"What? Do I look bad? I knew I should have worn my regular clothes." I clasp my hands tightly together, trying to think what else I could wear.

"It's not that Leo, I promise!" Neens says.

"Hijo . . ." my mom whispers.

"Mom?"

"You look so handsome." Her eyes start to water and she raises a hand to her mouth.

"Oh." I'm taken aback by both their reactions. I never really let myself believe I'm handsome. My mom has told me I'm handsome before, and I would just let it slide because she has to say that to me. She's my mom, that's what moms do. The look in their eyes makes me turn around and look at myself in the full-length mirror hanging on the wall. For once, I truly see myself and see something I haven't seen in a while.

Joy.

My mom comes up next to me and looks at me in the mirror, giving me a soft smile. Turning me to face her, she puts her hand on my cheek and I lean into her touch. "You, my son, are worthy of love. Now, go enjoy this date. I can't wait to hear all about it later tonight at dinner."

Before I can respond, there is a knock and we both head to the door. My heart is racing a mile a minute, and all I can do now is enjoy this moment with Ryder. I have my hand on the doorknob when I freeze,

"Leo, you got this, remember that you are in control of your emotions, not the other way around," Neens says from behind my mom.

I take a deep breath, inhaling and exhaling for a moment. She's right. I got this. I turn the knob, letting the door open, and reveal the most beautiful man of my life.

He looks me up and down, from head to toe, and his face forms a soft smile as his eyes meet mine. "Hi, handsome."

Chapter Seventeen

Ryder

My date with Leo is tomorrow and I want to make it perfect. My only problem is that I don't know what to do around here. I haven't had a lot of time since the store opened and, when I do have free time, I'm either with Jenni, talking about the shop, or with Leo.

Jenni and I are having lunch at my place—to talk about the shop, yet again—when I realize she is the perfect person to help me. I haven't spoken to her about Leo, but I have a feeling she has her suspicions.

"Hey Jenni, can I ask you something?" I ease the question in when there's a break in our back-and-forth of shoptalk.

"Huh? Oh, yeah. Go ahead."

"If one was going on a first date with someone, where would you recommend they take them?"

Jenni's eyebrow shoots up. "Is this for a friend or yourself, Ryder?"

"Okay fine . . . it's for me," I admit. "I need some good date ideas near here."

"Is this for the bookstore owner, Leo?" She smirks at me as I feel my face get red from embarrassment.

"How did you know?"

"Ryder, it hasn't been hard to clock your attitude whenever he is around. I started noticing on the day of the opening, when you screamed hello to him in front of everyone."

I laugh nervously, rubbing the back of my neck. "I did do that, didn't I?"

I look up at Jenni and our eyes meet. There's a slight smile on her face but I notice something in her eyes that makes me worry for a moment. She looks at me, then looks down at the table, responding, "Sure did. It was the day I noticed I had no chance with you."

It was as if all the air in my lungs is kicked out of me as I replay the words in my head.

I had no chance with you.

Then my brain restarts and I exclaim, "Wait! What are you saying right now? Do you like me? When did this happen?" I'm beginning to panic and Jenni lays her hand on my hand.

"Ryder, relax. Those feelings are long gone." She smiles at me, a little lopsided, but seems genuine. "On opening day, when I saw the way you were looking at Leo, I knew that it was more than just brewing a crush. It's okay."

I exhale loudly in relief. I rely on Jenni so much, if she were upset with me, I honestly don't know what we would do.

"Leo . . . he's such a good guy. He doesn't always see it, but he's gorgeous inside and out," I say, with a quick smile at Jenni. Thankfully, she smiles back. "I feel so comfortable around him . . . and have from the first time we met. It's . . . it's like the moment I looked into his eyes, I knew I belonged. To him. With him." I break off, blushing as I realize quite how much I'm opening up to Jenni—who just admitted she had been interested in me herself—but she just smiles softly at me.

"You're falling in love with him, aren't you?" she asks.

For a moment, I freeze, then the rightness of that statement hits me, hard. I close my eyes and take a deep breath, then look at Jenni as I confess, "Yes, I'm falling in love with him." My heart races, realizing that I've never said this out loud.

"Good. He seems like the perfect person for you," she says, giving me a light squeeze on my hand.

"Are we okay, Jenni?" I ask, frowning in concern. "I don't want you to think I'm pushing your feelings to the side."

"Like I said, Ryder, I've let my feelings die out. And anyway"—she grins, giving my hand a quick shake before letting it go—"I've been talking to someone else."

"Ohhh . . . Okay!" I let out a sigh of relief. "Wait, who is it?"

"Don't worry about that. Let's talk about this date," she insists, quickly changing the subject.

"Where do you think I should take him?

She smirks and gives me a wink. "I have the perfect idea."

I knock on Leo's door feeling calm and ready to start this date. I hear muffled voices on the other side of the door and wonder if everything is okay. I see the doorknob turn, and then the door opens and my eyes meet with Leo's beautiful brown eyes. I take Leo in as I take a mental picture, and I notice something is different about him. I trail my gaze down his body, then back up to his face. He looks so fucking sexy in this outfit. The way the shirt complements his tan skin and his eyes is so breathtaking, my heart skips a beat when he looks at me.

I'm falling in love with this man, and he doesn't know it. Yet.

I smile, saying softly, "Hey, Handsome."

Leo's face turns a soft red and smiles back at me, "Hello."

I turn to Leo's mom, hovering just behind his shoulder. "Hello, Mrs. Blanco, these are for you," I say, handing over the bouquet of hyacinths I brought with me.

"Oh, Ryder, these are so beautiful, you didn't have to do this!" she says and smiles broadly at the flowers.

"It's my absolute pleasure!" I assure her. "I was able to find a flower shop that has all different types of seasonal flowers. These caught my eye, and"—my gaze floats back to Leo—"the worker told me that the hyacinth flower represents a new beginning. I believe it's the perfect flower for this occasion."

Mrs. Blanco is beaming at me and Leo. "I've been told that once or twice," she agrees. "Thank you so much for this." She leans in for a hug and I hug her back with one arm.

Straightening up, I bring the other arm from behind my back. "And, this is for you, handsome," I say to Leo, handing him a single red rose with a note attached to the stem saying Happy Birthday.

"You didn't have to get me anything for my birthday, Ryder. You coming to dinner is more than enough." He reaches for the flower and our fingers touch. Our eyes meet and we look at each other for a moment, as our fingers rub on each other.

I lean in and kiss his cheek. "Who said that's all I have for you?"

I wink at him.

"Okay, that was smooth as fuck . . ." Nina interrupts the moment, and we all laugh.

"Hijo, let me take this and I'll make sure it gets water," Leo's mom tells him, reaching for his rose. "You boys go ahead on your date, we'll meet you back here for dinner."

"I forgot I didn't brush my teeth," Leo exclaims suddenly. "Let me do that quickly. Neens, can you come with me?" Leo asks, reaching out to grab Nina's arm.

"What the hell, I thought you—" Nina splutters, but Leo drags her away before she can finish.

Leo's mom and I chuckle.

"He won't take long. Make yourself comfortable, Ryder," Leo's mom tells me.

"I'm glad to have a moment with you. May I ask you something?"

"Of course! What's wrong?"

"Nothing is wrong, but I did wish your husband was here because I wanted to ask both of you." She smiles softly at me, giving me the courage to ask the question. "Your son has changed my life for the better. Every moment I'm with him it's like the world doesn't exist. He means so much to me, and I know he has a hard time loving himself at times. What I'm trying to say is that I'm in love with your son. With that, I wanted to have your approval to ask him to be my boyfriend?"

My heart is racing so fast I feel like I'm about to faint waiting for her answer.

Leo's mom smiles so big and her eyes start to water, "Ryder, you have shown my son what an inch of what love could be like, and with that I'm forever grateful to you. I know my husband will say the same. You have our approval."

My heart jumps for joy and the biggest smile comes to my face and I go in for a hug.

"Oh!" Leo's mom laughs as I pull her against me.

"Thank you! Thank you! This means the world to me! I promise to make sure he knows what love is."

"You better or I will hunt you down, Ryder!" She laughs.

I chuckle, "Yes ma'am!"

Leo and Nina return from the bathroom finding his mother and me hugging, "Are we interrupting something?" Nina teases.

Leo's mom turns around, wiping a tear from her eye, "No! No! We were just talking, that's all."

"Mom, are you okay? Why are you crying?" Leo rushes to his mom's side, his brow furrowed with worry, his hands flying out to her shoulders.

"I'm fine, hijo, something was in my eye. Now go enjoy this date!"

He smiles and looks at me, "That's my plan!"

I reach my hand out, "Ready?"

"Ready."

Chapter Eighteen

Leo

BEING BLINDFOLDED DOESN'T HELP with my anxiety at all, but Ryder wanted to keep our date a surprise. I didn't want to ruin anything, so I went along with it.

"So, do I get any hint?" I ask nervously.

"Nope!" Even though I couldn't see anything I knew from the tone of that response Ryder was smiling.

"That's not fair, it's my birthday. I should know what's happening, sir!"

"They call it a surprise for a reason."

"I guess you're right. How long till I can take this off?"

"Not long!" Ryder exclaims, then the car suddenly stops, and the engine switches off. "Let me help you out real quick!"

His car door opens and closes. I hear Ryder walking to my side and opening the door for me.

"Give me your hand and watch your step baby."

Hearing him calling me baby still gives me the biggest butterflies and I don't see it going away.

"Don't let me fall, okay?"

Grabbing my hand, he helps me out of the car, saying, "You will never fall with me around." But little does he know I'd already fallen. For him.

"Okay! Stand still so I can take off the blindfold."

"Okay," I smile, my body buzzing at having Ryder close to me.

I feel Ryder's hands on my arms sending goosebumps all over my body. He leans into my ear and whispers, "Before I take this off, there's something I haven't said yet."

Having his warm breath hit my skin makes all my hair stand, sending another shiver up my spine.

"What's that?" I whisper back.

"Happy Birthday, baby," he says in a deep, raspy voice that electrifies every muscle in my body. He then tilts my head and kisses my neck from behind. I let out a soft moan as I reach behind me to grab Ryder's thigh and grip onto his pants. He grunts as he pushes his cock on my ass and, the moment he does, I go crazy. I turn around and grab him by the shirt and pull him into a heated kiss. Blindfold on, I kiss him like I never had before. Our lips glide on top of each other sending surges of heat all over our bodies. His tongue fills my mouth in all the right places. It takes me a moment to remember that we are making out wherever we are, and I don't know where that is or who might be around us. I slow the kiss and bite his lower lip gently, before backing away.

For a moment we stand there, composing ourselves after that heated moment, trying to catch our breath "That was . . ." I take a deep breath in and exhale, "Amazing."

"More than amazing, it was breathtaking."

"Mm-hmm," I giggle.

"Looks like we found a kink, no?" Ryder says, his hand gently stroking my upper arm.

"Absolutely!" I smirk.

"Now, let's take this off and get this date going." He reaches behind my head and unties the blindfold. It takes me a moment to adjust to the sunlight and as my eyes focus they find Ryder's eyes.

"Now that's a beautiful sight to behold!" I laugh.

"My view is better for sure. Are you ready to find out where we are?"

He turns me around and I look at the building, with the sign that says *Wicks and Chicks.*

"Is this a candle-making place?!?" I squeal and jump around to see his face. Ryder laughs at my reactions, and it fills my heart with joy. "How did you know I've always wanted to do this? I've been asking Neens to come with me for months, but never had the chance to!"

"I may have had a little birdy on my shoulder."

"This is so perfect Ryder. Thank you!"

"Anything for you, birthday boy!"

We were ready to start our candles after learning more about different types of scents and waxes, but the first thing we needed to do was find something to make our candle in.

"What do you think we should do, Ryder?" I ask, looking around the shelves. There's no response and I turn around to look for Ryder, but I don't see him anywhere nearby. "Ryder?" I hiss, trying to not attract attention to myself. Confused and lost, I turn back to the front, but I'm not paying enough attention and someone on their way out, with a backpack, bumps into me and I lose my balance. I start to fall backward until I am caught by strong arms and pulled quickly into Ryder's chest.

"Baby! Are you okay? You should be more careful!" he whispers as I look up at him. We stare at each other for a moment, and I'm taken back to the very moment when we first met at the bookstore a few weeks ago. The world is at a standstill as his eyes look into mine just like they did that very first day. I nod, letting him know that I'm okay, and I steady myself in his arms.

"Seems like you are falling for me again?" His lips are inches from mine asking to be kissed. I keep my composure, trying to find my words.

"I'll always fall for you, knowing you'll be there to catch me," I say softly, meeting his gaze.

"Forever and always." He smiles at me, making my heart flutter. "Are you ready to make the candles?"

"Yeah, that's how I got myself in this predicament. I was looking for you, but I'm not mad I fell into your arms." I wink at him, aiming for flirtatious, but just making myself feel extremely awkward. "Oh god, that was so bad, wasn't it?"

Ryder bites his lower lip and leans into my ear "If you keep that up, I'm going to have to take you to one of these closets and have my way with your lips, got it?"

I feel my face get hotter, his deep voice making my knees weak. "I understand," I managed to get out. "Where were you anyways? I was looking for you."

"I'm sorry, I went to ask if they had these for us." He lifts his hand, and I finally notice he is holding two coffee mugs. "I was thinking we could make each other a candle. Something to light when we are missing one another and be reminded that we are always near each other."

This man is making me feel so loved I don't know what I did to deserve this. "Ryder, that is the sweetest thing anyone has asked me to do. I would love to make you a candle. This is the best birthday ever, thanks to you."

"The day isn't over just yet! Let's get these candles going, okay?" He smiles, grabbing my hand and leading us to our candle station. "Okay, you stay on this side and I'll stay on the other. Make whatever scent you want for me, and I'll do the same for you. Sound good?"

"Perfect!" I smile wide, excited to make something for the man I'm head over heels for.

About twenty minutes later I do the final step for Ryder's candle and then set it aside to check on Ryder. "How is the candle coming?" I ask, looking over to him and seeing how focused he is as he makes sure not to mess up the label.

He looks at me from the corner of his eye, "Don't take another step handsome!" he says in a faux-stern voice, but he can't keep it up. "This is going to be a surprise!"

I giggle and return to my spot. "Okay, my candle is set. I'm ready whenever you are!"

"Mine's ready, let's get them into boxes and head to your next surprise!"

"Another one? You don't need to do anything more, Ryder. This was amazing."

"Hush! Hush! Your birthday is a special day. You need more than one surprise!" His smile is so huge it makes me giggle at how adorable he is.

"Okay fine! I'm excited to see what is next."

Ryder pays for the candles and we head out to the car. As I put on my seatbelt, Ryder holds out the blindfold in front of my face.

"Not this again!" I exclaim. "You know how it makes me feel!"

"Oh, I know exactly how it makes you feel." He winks at me, "However, the next surprise won't be a surprise without it!"

I grab the blindfold, bringing it to my face, and everything around me goes dark. Instead of feeling anxiety, I felt joy.

Chapter Nineteen

Ryder

THE DATE IS GOING very well, but this next surprise is making me very nervous. My palms are sliding all over the steering wheel from being anxious. I want this all to go according to plan, and so far it is. The candle shop was amazing and seeing Leo's face light up from all the excitement made this worthwhile. Little does he know I'm about to ask him two very important questions in a matter of minutes.

"You're not peeking, *right?*" I ask, waving my hand over Leo's face to make sure he isn't looking.

"Nope! I'm being a good boy."

Something about him saying that phrase—*good boy*—makes my cock jerk with excitement.

"Mmm, good." I reach over and squeeze his thigh.

He reaches for my hand, takes it, and pulls it up to his lips, giving me a soft kiss that sends goosebumps up my arms.

"Are you ready for the next part of our date?"

"I'm ready!"

I get out of the car and head to the back, grabbing what I need, before helping Leo out. I open the door and help him out slowly so he won't trip or bang his head.

"Thank you," he says, holding onto my hand.

"Of course, handsome! Now watch your step here."

"Where are we going?" he asks, but I ignore that. I let go of his hand and walk a few steps ahead. Under the blindfold, Leo's face creases in confusion and he takes some tentative steps forward. "Ryder? Where did you go?"

"Stop right there!"

"Oh, okay!"

"Now take off the blindfold!"

Leo unties the blindfold and rubs his eyes to adjust them to the light. It takes him a moment to notice what is in front of him and where we were. I stand a few feet away from him, with a picnic basket in hand, at the bridge where we first kissed.

Leo rushes up to me and locks our lips in a passionate kiss, one of his hands sliding round my waist. The basket falls to the ground as I cup Leo's face to kiss him deeper.

Leo pulls back. "You—" he starts and goes in for another kiss. "Don't understand—" He kisses me again. "How much this means to me!"

I smile against his mouth as he kisses me more and more, then pull away slightly. "I love all the kisses, but do you want to set up the picnic?"

"Yes! Let's do it!"

We set up the blanket on the bridge and I set out all the finger foods I brought for us. I watch Leo as he helps me, taking in the moment. The sunlight warms our bodies, and a light breeze lifts Leo's curls. The waterfall makes a calming noise and the sound of the leaves on the trees moving in the breeze adds to the gentle buzz around us, blocking out any sounds of the city. This moment right now is everything and more.

We settle on the blanket, and I offer Leo a tub of chopped fruit, as I ask, "Are you ready to exchange candles?"

"Oh! Yes!" His eyes shoot wide open "I almost forgot about them!" he confesses.

I laugh from the pit of my stomach, "You are so fucking cute baby."

He smiles at me, looking up through those thick lashes, as I grab both the candles out of the basket and set them on the blanket.

"How do you want to do this?" I ask. "Both open them at the same time or one at a time?"

"Let's do them one at a time!"

"Sound's good! You go first then, birthday boy!" I say, nudging a candle wrapped in tissue paper towards him. Leo unwraps the candle that I made and turns it around to read the label.

"Crush," he reads, lifting his head to look at me, his brow furrowed slightly in thought.

I watch him in delight, seeing the wheels turn in his head.

"Crush, like the name of your store?"

"Mm-hmm!" I smile at Leo "And the scent is coffee with a hint of vanilla cream."

He sniffs the candle and smiles, closing his eyes for a moment. "This smells just like you, when I visit your shop. This is perfect! I think we were thinking the same when making our candles."

"What do you mean?"

"Check your candle out," Leo says, leaning in to sniff the candle again.

I grab the other candle, pulling the wrapping off, and turn it so I can read the label. "Pages." I look back at him, shocked by the realization, "Like the name of your store! How did we know to do this?" I say, smiling.

"We are connected. I'm not shocked we thought the same thing to do but give it a sniff."

I smell the candle. "Is there a hint of vanilla?"

"Yes!" he giggles. "Crazy, right?"

"A good type of crazy," I murmur.

"I didn't know how to make a scent that smells like a bookstore, but vanilla is the scent we use for my store, so I thought to use it for your candle."

We smile at each other, making the moment sweeter.

"I have one more thing to give you," I tell Leo, tucking the candle he made for me back in the basket.

"Ryder . . . you've done so much already . . ."

I pull out a black jewelry box and lay it on the blanket. He looks at me uncertainly, his gorgeous brown eyes looking like honeycomb from the way the sun is hitting them.

"I've been keeping this from you for a while now and I wanted the perfect gift for you. In this box is the memory of the very first time we met. A moment I'll never forget."

Leo reaches for the jewelry box, murmuring, "Ryder . . . you didn't have to . . ."

"Open it, baby!"

Leo opens the box and reveals a silver bracelet with a music code engraved on a silver plate. He looks up at me, brows knit in confusion, as I take the bracelet and put on his wrist.

"Scan the code with your phone."

Still looking confused, he slides his phone out of a pocket, clicks on his camera app, and scans the code. A moment later, "I Guess I'm in Love" by Clinton Kane starts playing. I stand up and reach my hand out to Leo.

I can't process what I'm doing right now. This man looking up at me has captured my soul, my heart, my world, and I never thought I'd be taking this risk. This leap. The fear of rejection lingers, like the ghosts of my past, but I know in my heart that he'll take my hand. I know this is real. He is my one. I guess I'm in love.

"Dance with me?"

Chapter Twenty

Leo

I STARE AT HIS hand, my heartbeat racing in my ears. Maybe I misheard him. Did he really ask me to dance with him? I tentatively take his hand. This is the moment I've been waiting for. It's what I've dreamed of, but is it too good to be true? Does a man like Ryder truly want to open up to someone like me? I let him guide me to the center of the bridge, my thoughts stringing and combining and overflowing like the music coming out of my phone.

"Is this . . . ?" I manage to whisper.

"The song playing the moment I caught you?" Ryder smiles softly, washing my entire body with a sense of calmness, sending all doubts away. "Yes, it is."

He remembered. He felt it. The connection that was flowing through our bodies the moment we touched. It wasn't in my head, and now I know I wasn't the only one.

"I don't know what to say . . ."

"You don't need to say anything, baby. Just know that since the moment my skin touched yours, I've belonged to you. You are becoming my world, my heart, and"—he puts his forehead on mine—"the man I love."

And just like that, all my doubts rush back in and I take a step back from Ryder. "You love me? Why me? No one could love someone like me. You shouldn't love me, Ryder."

"Leo, stop that!" he says sharply and I freeze "I don't believe one word you just said. You are loveable, more than loveable actually! You shine as you walk into a room, making everyone happier the moment they see you. I witnessed it with Mrs. Johnson the day you visited me. You, Leo. My Leo. Are worth it all."

I stand in front of a man willing to give me his entire heart to love me. This is all I've needed to hear, but the fear is lodged in my heart. I know I can't let fear hurt me anymore. He is reassuring me of the love he has for me. I need to choose to be happy, and I can be with Ryder. I step into him, laying my head on his shoulder as he wraps his arms around me again, and I softly whisper, "I'm scared."

Ryder hugs me tightly as I feel his heart racing against me. "I'm scared too, baby. Love is not easy, but with the right person love can grow into something magical."

I lift my head, looking up into Ryder's eyes. He cups my face with his hands and rests his forehead on mine. A tear forms and rolls down my cheek, hitting his fingers.

"Leo, this right here is the truest of love. I know you believe in us because, if you didn't, you wouldn't be standing here." He wipes the tears off my face, making me open my eyes to see he is also crying.

"I do," I finally admit to him.

"Then be with me officially. Be my boyfriend. I already feel I belong to you—all we need is the title. Leo Blanco, will you be my boyfriend?"

It's happening.

The moment I've craved since I first looked into this man's eyes. If he is taking this leap of faith, then I should do the same. "Yes," I say softly.

With a rush of pure love running in my body, I kiss my boyfriend for the first time. The kiss is filled with passion and heat. Our tongues dance. The world fades around us as we take each other in and never let go.

This day has been one of the best days of my life and I haven't stopped smiling since the park, all through dinner with my parents and Neens. At the end of the night, I walk Ryder to his car, holding hands. It feels so natural for us to be like this with each other.

"Ryder?"

"Yes, baby?" he says stopping in front of his car. I love the way he calls me *baby* so easily.

"Thank you for tonight. All of this has been amazing. You're amazing. I'm so happy to be your boyfriend."

He leans in, giving me a soft kiss on the lips. "You deserved it. I'm glad your birthday was good. However, I do have one last thing to ask you."

"Oh . . . what's that?"

"Will you be my date to the masquerade ball?"

I smile at Ryder. "I'll be your date forever and always," I venture.

We lean in as our lips come together in the sweetness of kisses. The perfect way to end a birthday.

As we part, Ryder whispers, smirking, "I can't wait to see you in those tights!"

Oh.

Yes.

Ryder has been excited to go the ball since it will be his first in Mapleton. I stopped going soon after high school started. Neens was popular so she was asked to go every year, but there was no point for me to be there, so why go? I'm excited that this year I'll be with my boyfriend. The only downfall is that this year's theme is Regency-inspired. Meaning the clothes are very layered and tight. Being a bigger boy, things like fittings can be difficult.

Oh, well. Neens will help me. And maybe I can get her to wear a ballgown.

And I get to go to the ball with my Ryder.

My boyfriend.

Chapter Twenty-One

Ryder

PUTTING THE CAR IN park as I get to Jenni's house, I check the time on my phone. The ball starts in about an hour and I'm picking up Jenni before heading over. Originally, I wanted to pick up Leo and take him myself. But Nina wanted them to enjoy getting ready together, so we agreed to meet on the dance floor. I can't wait to have my boyfriend in my arms tonight, and dance like no one is around. *Boyfriend*. It's still crazy to me that Leo and I are together.

We came up with a game: we didn't tell each other what we were wearing or what our masks looked like. Leo said he wanted to embrace the theme and see how our connection can guide us to one another. Honestly, I don't doubt that the moment I lay eyes on him I'll know it's him. There's a knock on my window and I turn to see Jenni, waiting for me to let her in. "Oh, shit. My bad Jenni!" I say, unlocking the doors.

"Damn, Ryder, you okay? I was standing there for a minute."

Rubbing the back of my neck, I say, "Yeah! I mean, I want this night to be perfect for Leo. He never does stuff like this, and I was the one to push him. I don't want this to hurt what we're building, you know?"

"Hey—it'll be okay. Remember that you both want to be there, together. It's another step in your relationship. Have fun and show Leo how much his coming with you means."

She was right. Tonight is about us and getting to explore more of our feelings. I'm not going to let my nervousness get to me. "Thank you, Jenni. It's going to be a fun night. Speaking of fun . . . don't you have a date? When do I get to meet this mysterious man of yours?"

Jenni just rolls her eyes at me. She's been busy of late, and on her phone a lot. I hope whoever this person is, they treat her with the respect she deserves.

"We'd better get a move on if you want to make it there before Leo. I didn't rush myself to sit in front of my house."

"Just tell me one thing . . . are they going to be there?" She looks away, but I saw her start to blush.

"Ohh! Does that mean yes?!" I tease, starting the car. "I'm keeping a lookout!"

"Ryder, respectfully . . . I hate you!"

As we pull into the parking lot, I see the people in their Regency-inspired outfits walking inside, making me more excited to see Leo in his. Jenni and I walk in with each other, taking in the venue and decorations. Mapleton goes all out. It's like they took a scene right out of a book, transporting us to the early 19th-century Regency period into a story of romance and class.

"This place is insane, Jenni," I lean in to speak to Jenni.

"Mapleton is known for its big events! That's one of the main reasons I'm part of the town's committee."

"Wait? Huh? How did I not know this? You are always at the shop though . . . how do you have time for all this?"

"It's called days off, Ryder."

"I mean—yeah I know, but still."

"I have a life outside of the shop. We may be close, but you don't know everything."

Jenni has a point. We don't share much—and maybe we'd be even better friends if we did. "Hey, listen, Jenni," I say, turning to face her. "You're my best friend, and I want our bond to grow."

She nods, with a soft smile.

My eyes are suddenly drawn to the stairs on the other side of the dance floor. Lifting my head, I see a man wearing a royal blue tailcoat, over a cream vest and ruffled top. Gold accents line his coat, with buttons that are a darker shade of gold. His cream-colored mask covers his tan skin, but his curls fall in front of his eyes, framing the shape of his face. "Excuse me," I say to Jenni.

"Where are you going? Ryder?"

It's like my body is working on its own as my legs move to the dance floor. The man in blue and I lock eyes as he starts walking down the stairs. The heat rises within me the closer I get to him. With every step, my heart beats faster and faster.

It's him.

My hand reaches out for him, and I wait to see what he will do.

Chapter Twenty-Two

Leo

As I watch my mom and Neens run around the house, getting ready for the ball tonight, I'm just trying to process what I'm about to do. I never go to these types of events. Putting myself out there isn't who I am, but I promised Ryder and Neens that I'd give it a chance.

"Leo! What are you doing?! We need to leave in an hour—go get ready!" Neens snaps me out of my thoughts.

"I'm going! Calm your ass!" I yell back at her as I leave the living room.

"If I could, I would! Now hurry up! If you need help let us know."

"Will do!" I say, heading to grab a quick shower. I find myself again looking at myself in the mirror and noticing that I don't feel that darkness I used to. Taking a deep breath, and letting it out slowly, I smile at myself as I let go of those thoughts and get dressed for the ball.

"Leo! Come out already, we want to see you!" Both Neens and my mom are yelling to hurry me up.

"I'm almost done!" I add gel to my hair, making my curls pop out more so they can frame the shape of my face, and then head to the living room to find both my parents and Neens dressed and waiting. They all turn as I walk in, smiling, making me feel so loved.

"Hijo, you look . . . I don't have the words to say how proud I am of you," my dad says in a soft voice.

"My baby looks like a fine proper gentleman, doesn't he, my love," my mom says to my dad.

"He certainly does, mi amor," he replies, putting his arm around her shoulders.

"Can you guys stop being so sappy?" I comment. "You both look amazing as well." I smile at them and turn to Neens, only to see that she is tearing up.

"Nina? What's wrong?" I rush to her. She shakes her head and grabs a few tissues that are nearby.

"It's nothing"—she blows her nose—"there are tears of joy, Leo. You're coming out of your shell and doing these things you said you never would do. You're my best friend and I love you so much, Leo. All I want is the best for you. I'm so happy to see you grow."

"Nina . . . Stop it right now. You're going to make us both cry." I grab her, hugging her tightly, as I whisper in her ear, "I love you too."

I take in the moment, thinking it's one of the best of my life. Having my parents and Neens with me as I truly open myself, to not only a man but to the world as well, means so much.

"It's getting late, guys. Let's get going before there's no parking!" my mother says quickly and ushers us out.

At the venue, I feel my anxiety build as we head into the ballroom, each breath becoming harder as I break into a sweat under all the formal layers. I stop for a moment to catch my breath before entering. My parents and Neens turn to look at me.

"You guys go ahead, I'll stay here with Leo for a moment," Neens says to my mom.

"You sure honey? I can . . ."

"It's okay Mom, I just need a moment," I say in between breaths. "Go enjoy yourselves, you both deserve it. I love you both."

My parents come up to me and hug me and, with that, I feel calmer.

"Want a second to relax?" Neens asks me.

"I think I'm just freaking out about what others will think."

"Think about what? You? Let them think about you, Leo. You will blow all these people away. They will finally see what I have seen in you all these years."

"What's that?"

"Love. Pure love. You shine when you spread your love. When you walk into that room tonight, they will see the person I love the most. Don't let those emotions take this moment away from you, okay?"

I took my family and Neens for granted. I'm so lucky to have them in my life. "Okay," I smile at Neens. She smiles back at me, grabbing my hand and leading me to what could be the best night of my life.

As we enter the ballroom, I look around and take in the details of the ballroom. The way the dancers move in unison, swaying back and forth and twirling around the dance floor. Dresses moving so elegantly as the women twirl around to different partners. The men dancing as if they are gliding from one person to another. The dance floor is framed with columns in an oval shape, with flowers roping around the tops of the columns bringing it all together. I'm speechless at the scene that's in front of me.

"Ready?" Neens asks, before we walk down the stairs.

"I'm ready." I take a deep breath and look forward.

My heart starts to beat at a quicker pace as I walk down the stairs. As I look around the crowd, my eyes fixate on a man wearing a maroon coat with a black laced vest over a white dress shirt. His vest has maroon buttons that help highlight his torso in the sexiest way. An image of me ripping off the vest revealing his body rushes into my head. My eyes find themselves moving up his body to his bare skin that is showing above his dress shirt. I scan his neck to his black mask, finding his eyes staring right at me. I lick my lips trying to wake myself from this dream. The need to kiss his lips. The draw to this man. His dirty blond hair with a hint of ginger is perfectly styled with a strand falling in front of his gorgeous face. My pull to him is too strong to stop. I am pulled like a magnet down the stairs and across the room, stopping only a few feet from this man.

It's him.

I stare into his eyes, my body on fire wanting to reach for him.

He reaches out. "May I have this dance?" he asks, with a rasp in his voice that makes my body shiver. I pick up my hand to reach out, but then hesitate.

No, Leo. Don't let fear stop you.

Our fingers are inches away from each other. Our eyes meet again, and I place my hand in his.

"You may."

He bows as he brings my hand to his lips, giving it a gentle kiss. He lifts his eyes to me, his lips still on my skin. and the darker shade of blue of his eyes is intoxicating. He pulls me in, taking my breath away as I land in his arms. Dancers spin around us in unison as the music starts at an upbeat tempo.

"You trust me?" he asks.

I nod. He looks at me with a soft smile and raises his hand to his mask, taking it off.

"Ryder," I say with a sigh of relief. I knew it was him, but seeing his face fully was what I was waiting for.

"Hi, Leo," he smiles, lifting his hand to my cheek. Over his shoulder I notice people are staring.

His hand moves to my mask, and I grab it, frozen from fear of our bubble disappearing. His eyes go soft as he looks at me, reassuring me that this will be okay.

"It's you and me, my love. Focus on me. Focus on us," he says in a soft voice as he takes my mask from my face.

"Keep looking at me," Ryder instructs, as his finger grazes my chin. He leans in, giving me a soft gentle kiss.

"There's my Leo," he whispers into my lips. "Follow my lead, okay?"

Before I can answer Ryder pulls me in, and we join the dancers around the dance floor. The music sends a surge of energy through me and my body feels free. All eyes seem to be on Ryder and me, but we dance around the room as if the rest of the world is nonexistent. I smile bigger than I ever have before, knowing that I've completely fallen in love with this man. With every step I take my confidence grows. My entire life I've wanted a moment where I knew I was worthy of what life can give me. At this moment, as I'm dancing in front of the entire town, I feel the old me fading away with each spin I take.

This is who I am.

This is the Leo I wanted to be.

Who I have always been.

As I take one last spin, I land right back into the arms of the love of my life.

Both of us breathing heavily, we stare into each other's eyes. I grab Ryder's hand and pull him off the dance floor. Turning to face him, I blurt out, "Kiss me." With no hesitation, our lips crash into each other. The kiss is heated with passion and want. A soft moan comes from my throat as Ryder slides his tongue over mine.

The sound of someone clearing their throat behind me makes us jump apart.

"Quite a show you boys are giving," Mrs. Johnson smirks at us. My body goes warm as I realize what we were doing in front of everyone. Mrs. Johnson walks up to us, grabs our hands and joins them together. Holding our hands together she looks up at us. "My sweet young boys, this right here is love. Don't ever let it go. Cherish it with your entire being."

Ryder and I look at one another and smile softly.

Mrs. Johnson looks at Ryder. "Remember what I said to you that day. Don't run from this." She smiles up at me, and says, "I'm so proud of you both. You showed tremendous bravery and strength." With that, she lets go of our hands and walks to her husband who is waiting for her a few feet away. He gives us a wink before he walks his wife out of the ballroom.

"That was . . ." I say.

"Perfect." Ryder turns to me, laying his hand on my cheek.

I smile at him, "Yes, you are."

Ryder laughs as he rubs my face with his thumb. He looks around the ballroom, asking, "Have you seen Jenni? I kinda just walked away from her when I saw you."

"Oh, no. I did the same thing to Neens when I saw you," I say.

"Let me go find her real quick. I won't take too long I promise."

"Take your time, Ryder. I gotta find Neens as well."

"Well looks like I found you first," Neens says from beside me.

"What the fuck!" I yelp. "Don't scare me like that!" Ryder and Neens laugh at my reaction. "It's not funny you two. She scared me."

"Baby, your face was priceless!" Ryder says.

"Not my fault you're easy to scare," Neens says, smirking.

"You know what . . . have you seen Jenni?" I ask.

Neens face goes from calm to worried. She seems a little flushed as well. I stare curiously at my best friend. What on earth is going on?

"I don't know where she would be. Why would I know?" Neens rambles.

"Are you okay? Why do you look flushed? Where were you?" I interrogate Neens.

"Leo, what is with all the questions?" Neens spits out quickly. "I don't know where she is, okay?"

"Okay! Sorry for asking." I shake my head.

"I'll look for her," Ryder says. "Don't go anywhere, I still want to dance with you."

"I'll be waiting."

Ryder walks away from Neens and me. I watch him leave and, the moment he does, I already want him back in my arms. I shake off the impulse to follow him and focus on the swirling dancers. Some familiar faces, some anonymous behind their masks. All dressed to the nines in Regency-inspired outfits. This really is something. Though, now I'm not focused on Ryder, I realize how warm the tight layers of clothing and the press of the crowd make me.

"You want a drink?" Neens asks.

"Yeah, I'll take one," I tell her with a smile.

"I'll be right back!" she tells me as she turns to head to the bar.

I find a seat at the nearest table that isn't being used. I notice people looking at me and my heartbeat picks up, my chest getting tight. I try my best to keep the negative thoughts out of my head. I try to calm my breathing.

"Look who's out of his book cave. I guess bears do wake up from hibernation," someone whispers in my ear.

I get up quickly from my seat. *That voice.* The voice that put me down for many years of my childhood.

"Alli," I say flatly, turning to face her.

"Hello, Bear," Alli says, with a wicked smile.

"Stop calling me that. Aren't we a little old to be acting like children?"

"Look who thinks they have a backbone now," she says, laughing cruelly. "You'll always be that weak kid who can't handle anything without his little friend. Where is she anyway? I would love to see Thing One and Thing Two back together."

Alli Brooks was my worst nightmare growing up. The downfall of living in a small town is that your class is stuck together until you graduate. Alli found any way to make my life a living hell with name calling or pranking me. The worst thing she ever did was pay the guy I had a crush on to ask me on a date. I was newly out of the closet, and I was so excited to go on my first date. Neens was out of town that weekend. I went to meet up with him at the spot we agreed to and, when I got there, I was greeted by all the popular kids. Frozen with fear, I didn't know what was happening until Alli walked out, telling me how it was a prank to see if I would fall for him. She said that trash like me would never find love in this world and got the older jocks to throw me in a dumpster.

As I laid in the dumpster, I heard everyone laugh at me. I was too scared to get out and run. I felt so powerless. All I could do was cry and wait it out. After what seemed like hours, I got out and walked back home.

Ever since that day, I have kept to myself and never bothered to do anything school or town related. Neens doesn't even know what happened.

"What do you want, Alli?" I grumble.

She walks closer to me, but I stand my ground. I'm not going to let her win this.

"You seem very smitten with Ryder, don't you?" she taunts as she gets closer to me.

How does she know who Ryder is?

"How do you know him?" I ask, with worry in my voice.

"You don't need to worry about that, Bear" She smirks at me "What you should worry about is if what you think is going on between you two is real."

My heart is racing. What is she trying to say?

"What are you talking about?"

Alli walks around me and I turn to follow her.

"Someone like Ryder would never like a weak bear like you."

My hands start to shake.

"Face it, Bear. You're fat and ugly. Ryder is hot and belongs with someone hot like me."

My legs feel weak.

"Wasn't it a little too easy to fall for him?"

I lose my breath.

"Hmmm . . . seems like you are catching on to what I'm saying." Alli gets close again and whispers in my ear, "All of this was a lie. You are nothing to him. You aren't worthy of anything."

I push her away from me "You're lying! You don't know him!"

This can't be happening again.

She laughs. "Bitch, look around you! You don't belong in this world. You're nothing but an ugly bear."

The room is spinning around me. I need to get out of here. I run past Alli trying to find my way out, bumping into people as I do. They look at me and all I see is disgust in their eyes.

She's right, I don't belong here. No one wants me. Ryder doesn't love me. This was all a lie.

I can't breathe.

I frantically look around for a way out. I see an exit door and run as fast as I can.

Chapter Twenty-Three

Ryder

As I look around the ballroom for Jenni, I feel like I'm walking on clouds. Being with Leo on the dance floor in front of the town felt like magic. I need to find Jenni quickly, as I don't want to miss another second of this night with Leo. The only thing I can use to find her is her bright yellow dress. I don't see a lot of other girls wearing that color so it should be easy to find her, but I can't. I head to the bathroom thinking maybe there is a line. As I turn into the hallway leading to the restroom, I bump into someone.

"Woah! I'm sorry!" I say, then realize who I bumped into "Jenni! There you are!"

"Damn, Ryder! Watch where you're going!" she yelps back at me.

"I've been looking for you for a while now. I left Leo waiting for me with Nina." I get a closer look at Jenni and realize she looks a little breathless, "Are you okay? You seem out of breath."

Jenni's face glows a dark shade of pink when I mention that to her.

"Oh! Yeah, I'm good," she says, as she fixes her dress which looks more wrinkled than it did when I picked her up.

"Okay, well you ready to head to Leo and Nina?"

Jenni nods to me, "Lead the way" she says as she tucks a piece of hair behind her ear.

We walk through the crowd of dresses and tailcoats, heading to where I left Leo and Nina. As we get closer, the crowd gets denser, and people seem to be trying to see what's going on ahead of us. I push through until I see Nina, her face furious, in the face of a random woman.

"What the fuck did you do, Alli! Where is Leo?!" Nina yells, as the woman smirks at her.

What does she mean? Where is Leo?

My heart starts to race as I look around and don't see the man who has my heart. I shove through the remaining crowd, ignoring the objections of the people round me, as I fight to get to Nina.

"What do you mean, where is Leo?" I ask, trying not to shout, then sucking in a deep breath. I have no clue what's happening, but Nina's fury is disconcerting. She's usually so sunny and calm, but this is a mama bear in protective mode.

"Look who it is," the strange woman drawls, interrupting me. "The man of the hour."

I look at her and she has a wicked smile that makes my blood boil. My fists are clenching convulsively at my sides and all the joy that had me walking on a cloud earlier is gone. I don't even know this woman and I already want her gone out of my sight.

"And who are you? What did you do to Leo?" I snarl, trying to make sense of what is going on.

"I'm Alli and don't worry about that low life, handsome." She sneers and runs her manicured nail down my coat.

"Hey! That's my—" Nina yells, but I put my hand out to stop her.

"I got this Nina," I say, keeping my eyes on Alli.

Nina nods at me as she takes a step back.

"I'll repeat myself one more time. What did you do to my boyfriend?"

Alli laughs at my question, making me even angrier, my hands balled into fists.

"It's funny that you're calling that creature a boyfriend. All you should know is that I got him out of our way. I've had my eyes on you since you first arrived, and that ogre—"

I rush to get closer to Alli "Watch what you say!" I let out, from my clenched teeth.

"Woah, slow your roll, sexy. I don't get physical till the second date, but for you, I'll break a rule or two," Alli says as she puts her hands on my chest.

I grab her icy hands and rip them off my body. No one will touch me like that other than Leo.

"I don't care what you think. You are nothing but a lonely person who loves to hurt people."

Alli stares at me with soulless eyes as she walks around my body with her hand touching me "How sad. I guess for someone to like trash they must be trash themselves."

"Get your ugly ass hands off me and tell me what you did to him!" I say, turning around to face Alli.

"I told him the truth. That he is nothing and that he will never be worthy of love."

From the corner of my eye, I see Nina with a piece of cake in her hand and anger in her eyes. I step back.

"Hey, Alli!" Nina yells.

Allie turns around and Nina smashes a piece of cake on Alli's face. Icing and cake spill onto her dress. Alli screams, "What the fuck!"

"Oh! I missed a spot," Nina says, rubbing even more cake on Alli.

"I'll help clean her off!" Jenni says as she picks up a drink and pours it over Alli's head.

The entire crowd starts to laugh at Alli including myself.

"Seems like others agree with me, sweetheart," I say as I wink at her.

Alli runs out of the crowd as frosting falls from her dress. I go up to Nina and Jenni, "Guys I need to find Leo. Do you have any idea where he would go?"

"Honestly, he doesn't go anywhere other than the bookstore or his house. I have to look for him too. Alli bullied him his entire life, and I thought he finally got over it."

"No, I got this, Nina" I say and I turn and run towards the exit.

It's raining, the dark and wet weather fitting with my mood, but not helping as I make a perfunctory search of the outside of the venue. There's no sign of Leo so I head to my car, pushing my dripping hair off my face.

As I speed down the road, all I can hear is the thumping of my own pulse and the thundering of the rain on the car's roof. My heart longs to find Leo, every second I can't feeling too long. To think he could be out in this weather alone and upset frightens me. I can only hope he is heading to the one place I can think of.

I'm probably driving too fast for these conditions, not caring that I could crash at any moment, only thinking of getting to him. I make the turn into the park, splashing mud all over my car. Unsurprisingly, the parking lot is deserted. The park, that is such an oasis in good weather, looks gloomy and uninviting in the dark and lashing rain. As I run to the bridge as fast as I can, the rain is so heavy that I can't see past a few feet in front of me.

"Leo!" I yell as I run. I need to find him. He has to be here. I rush to the bridge, swiping rain from my eyes, trying to get my vision as clear as it can be. As I get closer to the bridge, I see someone standing there and stop.

"Baby! Is that you?" I call, my chest heaving.

"Stop! Don't come closer, Ryder!" Leo yells.

Everything in me is screaming for me to move to him, "Baby, please . . ." I put my hands up and creep a little closer.

"Don't call me that! I need you to leave me alone," he says with a cold voice, not sounding like the Leo I danced with at all. Tears and raindrops spill down his face.

The rain goes from feeling heavy to sharp, as if the droplets turned into ice, from how cold Leo's voice sounds. "I'm not going anywhere, Leo! I belong here with you, and no one else!"

"I don't belong with anyone! I'm not good enough! Alli was right!" he screams at me and falls to his knees, his face in his hands.

I rush over to him and kneel before him, uncaring of the wet, dirty ground and how soaked we both are, and cup his face in my hands.

"Don't touch me!" he snarls, pushing my hands away, sending a wave of sadness over me.

"Leo . . ." I whisper, leaning closer.

"Get away from me!" He pushes me back, making me land on my butt. In shock at what is happening my eyes start to water, anger, sadness, and confusion fighting for the upper hand inside me.

What is happening to him? To us? Can I fix this?

Chapter Twenty-Four

Leo

I DIDN'T KNOW WHERE to go as I fled the ball. My legs just kept moving as if they were thinking on their own. The rain started and it got harder to see where I was going. Somehow, I made my way to the bridge where Ryder and I first kissed. This is the last place I want to be, but something drew me here. My head is a fog, with nothing but all the words Alli put in it, repeating over and over.

Fat.

Ugly.

You don't belong.

Tears fall down my face as I try to think clearly. I can't let someone ruin all the hard work I've put in these past few weeks. But the suggestions Alli made sneak in and hurt, so much. Was this all a lie? Is it too much to believe that someone like him could love someone like me?

"Leo!" I hear someone yell my name then, out of the corner of my eyes, I spot Ryder running towards me. "Baby! Is that you?" he calls as he comes to a halt. His beautiful outfit is soaked, just like mine, and his hair is dark with the wet, dripping down into his face.

"Ryder..." I whisper under my breath, and I see him take a step towards me. "Stop! Don't come closer, Ryder!"

He stops moving and I think I see his heart shatter as he tries to reach for me.

"Baby, please . . ." he says to me with a soft voice.

"Don't call me that! I need you to leave me alone." I say sharply and he visibly flinches.

"I'm not going anywhere, Leo! I belong here with you, and no one else!"

I feel weak, and I can't take this pain anymore. I fall to my knees as I scream "I don't belong with anyone! I'm not good enough! Alli was right along!"

My hands are over my face, but I feel as much as hear Ryder rushing to comfort me. He's in front of me, putting his hands on my cheeks, and with his touch my skin starts to burn with fire. I can't feel all this right now. I can't. It's too much. "Don't touch me!" I push his hands off me. With every rejection, I can see his love fade from his eyes.

"Leo . . ." He whispers trying to get closer, but I don't let him.

"Get away from me!" I lash out verbally and physically, pushing him with all the strength I have left in me. He falls backward and I bring my eyes up to look into his.

There it is.

The sadness I feel is reflected in his eyes—and I'm the one causing his pain. I look away so I won't see when Ryder realizes I'm not worth it and leaves.

"That's it!" Ryder gets back on his knees and grabs hold of me. "Look at me right now, Leo!" Moving his hands to my shoulders he shakes my body, but it could be happening to someone else.

"Just say it already," I mumble, not having the energy to speak louder. "I know you don't love me."

Ryder grabs my chin firmly, tilting my face towards his. Reluctantly, I look into his eyes. They are bluer than I've ever seen them. And what do I see shining from them?

Love.

Ryder tilts my chin and goes in for my lips, kissing me softly, then tugging slowly on my bottom lip before letting go and capturing my lips again. Our bodies breathe in unison as the kiss deepens and turns more passionate. The world around me fades, as all my senses focus on Ryder. His lips send fire through my body with every contact. The smell of his cologne hits me as we kiss harder. The sound of the rain fades away to nothing but silence. All I want is to stay in this moment forever.

Ryder stops the kiss and lays his forehead on mine as we both try to catch our breath.

"Why did you—" I take a breath, "stop?"

"Because, as much as I love to kiss you, I need you to know this isn't just physical for me." Ryder sighs, closing his eyes for a moment, then straightens up, bringing a sliver of space between our bodies. "I kissed you to show you that you can feel what I feel. To remind you that this—us—is the realest thing in my life. You are the only person I've ever loved, Leo. I think you are the love of my life. I need you to get that in your gorgeous head, baby."

I look at him trying to find the right words to say. His expression, his body language, it all looks sincere. But I don't trust myself to know what's real. The doubts are loud in my mind.

"Follow me," he says, rising to his feet and tugging me by the wrist.

"Where?" I ask, as I scramble awkwardly to stand. My clothes are soaked and now my breeches are filthy, but I'm barely aware of the cold and wet.

"Just follow me!" he says. I can't tell if that's exasperation in his voice or he's just trying to be heard over the rain.

My heart feels heavy. Ryder might have said he still loves me, but I'm frozen inside, just letting him urge me along the path through this torrential rain. We get to the parking lot and his Jeep sits alone under a streetlamp.

Ryder drops my hand and opens the backseat door for me, waving me inside. "Get in," he tells me.

A cold shudder runs down my body, but I don't know if it's him, me, or just because I am soaking wet. I sit down in the backseat, watch Ryder close my door and walk to the other side of the car. He climbs in the backseat with me, and we sit in silence for what feels like forever until I manage the strength to finally speak.

"Why did you bring me here?" I ask, realizing as I say it how stupid I sound.

He shifts his body to face me, "I didn't want you to get sick in the rain, and I needed you close to me."

As I take a deep breath, I lay my head on the headrest. I'm confused about why this man is still so loving to me after all that I said to him at the bridge. "Why?" I force out, my voice breaking slightly.

"What do you mean, Leo?" Ryder asks, turning to face me, and I feel his hand move to my thigh, grabbing my attention. I stare down at the strong hand on my sodden leg as he says, "Like I said on that bridge, you are the love of my life; whatever you say to me won't change that."

My eyes start to water as I let those words sink in. A tear forms, trailing down my cheek, but Ryder wipes it away with his thumb. I lean into his touch, wanting more. I know he is right, and all Alli said to me was a lie. I just wish my heart would believe in him over Alli or my own insecurities.

"What Alli did to you . . . was the lowest of the low," Ryder says slowly. "She knew what to say to you to upset you, and I'm sorry I wasn't there. I honestly can't believe a grown woman behaved so much like a petty playground bully. She got what she deserved at the ball."

"Wait—what?" I look up at him in confusion. "What happened?"

Ryder chuckles as he remembers. "Let's just say handling her with Nina was a piece of cake."

We both start to laugh. "You better tell me later," I mutter, wiping my eyes. That laugh helped. I feel lighter, less like the world is crushing my heart, even though I'm trembling with cold. I shake my head and whisper to myself, "I can't believe I let her do this to me again."

"Hey . . ." Ryder says, grabbing my hand. "Don't let some pathetic person with no life destroy what you have built. This-this could be something to learn from, yeah? Trust in yourself and the love you have," he sounds unsure about how I might take what he's saying. But he's right. He smiles at me and brings my hand to his lips, pressing a soft kiss to the back of my back. "Your hands are cold," he comments. He looks at me narrowly. "Baby, you're freezing! Take those clothes off, I have some blankets in the back."

I feel my face warm up at the idea of taking off my clothes before him. The last time I tried to take off my shirt in front of Ryder, I freaked out. But he is right: I'm freezing in these wet clothes. I take a deep breath. "Okay," I say softly and start to undress the layers of my outfit, thinking I can always leave my undershirt on.

Ryder reaches over the back seat grabbing two blankets. "If you don't mind, I'm going to get out of these clothes as well."

The tension in the Jeep grows as we both get undressed. Despite dealing with the intricacies of waistcoat buttons and a sodden necktie, I can't keep my eyes from floating to the view of him unbuttoning his shirt. His skin glows in the cold light of the streetlamp outside and my body starts to respond, heat swirling in my stomach. All I want is to touch every inch of him and rip his clothes off with my bare teeth. I watch as he starts to unbuckle his belt, then drag my gaze away.

"You okay, baby?" Ryder asks.

"Mm-hmm. Just trying to get warm," I tell him, undoing my pants and shuffling them under me. I can feel Ryder staring at my thighs as I pull my pants lower, and I can't work out if his focused gaze makes me feel uncomfortable or just appreciated.

"Here, put this around you," Ryder wraps the blanket around my body and pulls me close, rubbing my arms to warm me up. We lock eyes as the tension grows more and more. The heat within me is getting too much to handle. Ryder being this close to me makes every cell in my body go haywire. "Ryder . . ."

"Yeah?" he asks in a hoarse whisper.

I feel the heat from his breath inches away from my lips. With every breath, he sends waves of heat to my groin.

I need him. I need his touch. I grab him by the neck and push our lips into a kiss that opens a flood of pleasure all over me. My other hand finds its way onto his chest. I need more of him. So much more.

I let out a soft moan as he breaks the kiss and moves his lips to my neck, making my cock throb. I move my hand to his thigh, squeezing as he finds another spot that sends electricity down my spine to my groin, making me moan. My hand roams over his leg to his hard bulge and I stroke him there, feeling precum warm a patch on his damp boxer briefs. I grab his huge length, confined in his underwear, gasping as my hand is filled with his thickness.

I want it. No, I need it. I gently squeeze, asking "May I?"

"God, yes," Ryder rasps. "Please, baby."

He comes up from my neck, sending a rush of cold air over me as he sits back slightly. His eyes are dark with desire and need. I pull his underwear down at the front and I watch his face as his length springs out from its confines. He starts to breathe heavily as I rub the head of his cock with my thumb, I move my hand up and down his shaft as I watch him come undone.

"Ahh . . . yes . . . fuck . . ." he moans. With each moan, I feel my erection get harder and harder in my own damp underwear. I want him to know how much I love and want him.

"Can these seats lay down?" I ask Ryder, hinting at what I want to happen next.

"Yeah, they do. Do you want to lay down?"

"Yes . . ."

He smiles at me and turns his body to pull the lever to let the seats lie down. I immediately miss the warmth of his body near mine.

Ryder lies down on the reclined seats, holding his hand out to me to join him.

I shake my head slightly, whispering, "There's something I've been wanting to do for a while now."

"What's that?" Ryder asks, bringing his arms up under his head. He's all laid out, just for me.

"Let me show you," I say as I turn to face him fully. "These gotta go," I say, grabbing his boxer briefs and Ryder lifts his hips so I can take them all the way off, dropping them in the footwell.

My gaze fixes on his cock, noting every detail, like the way the tip shines from precum, and how it's dripping down his veiny shaft. I glance up to Ryder's face, noticing that he is staring at me, admiring it. I'm going crazy with lust and before I overthink everything my lips are on him. I go deep, inch by inch as the saltiness of his precum makes me crave him even more.

"Fuck! Leo!" Ryder moans, with a deep grunt. I love the feeling of validation from making him feel good, but I still need more, swallowing him down.

He grabs my head as I'm sucking and I let him take control. He pushes me up and down his length making me choke a little as I bottom out on his cock.

"Fuck, baby. Yes! Keep doing that . . . just like that . . ." Ryder is babbling above me as I deep throat him more and more. I grab his balls with one hand as the other is moving up and down with my mouth. I squeeze gently on his balls making him tense up as I make his cock wetter. "Fuck . . . come here, baby." He pulls me off him and up his body, our lips crashing into each other with an explosive kiss.

Shudders go through my entire body, making me moan from the back of my throat. His hands slide onto my thighs going up my body . . . and I tense up.

Ryder breaks the kiss and we pant into each other's' mouths for a moment before he says, "I know how you feel about your shirt being on. I don't want to force you to do anything you don't want to do."

I get teary again as I try to fight the feeling of needing to cover myself, needing to run, within me. He puts his hand on my cheek.

"You can trust me, Leo. You always can."

I nod at him letting him know I'm ready. I take a deep breath as he starts to take my undershirt off. I close my eyes, letting go of my fear. I feel the moment the shirt comes off and I take a moment, breathing deeply.

"Open your eyes, my love . . ." Ryder says, laying his forehead on mine.

I open my eyes to see Ryder looking at me with such a warm, loving expression. "There's my beautiful soulmate."

I did it. I fought my fear!

I never felt so free in my life. It feels like a breakthrough. In the back of this car, cocooned by curtains of rain, after the worst evening I've had in years. I didn't let my fear control me. I love Ryder. I'm head over heels in love with this man, and I need him to know. I smile softly knowing what I want to say next.

"I love you, Ryder. I'm so in love with you that I can't even think straight anymore. You are my person. You make me feel confident and strong. I need you right now."

Ryder's face glows with happiness as he processes what I just told him. "You . . ."

"Love you? Yes, I do!" I say laughing. "Now can we get back to what we've been doing?"

He smirks at me, "Lie down, it's my turn now."

I feel my face get warmer from how sexy he sounds. I lay myself down on my back and Ryder climbs on top of me. I bring my hands to his hips and let them explore every muscle from his ass to his shoulders. His naked dick is throbbing against me. He starts to kiss my neck and slowly moves down my body until he reaches my boxers, sliding a hand under the waistband to touch me. I shudder as he pulls my erection out and, before I can feel the cool air on it, he swipes his warm tongue over the tip, licking up precum that's dripping.

"Mmmm . . ." he groans, "you taste better than I imagined, baby."

He goes back for more, wrapping his lips around me and I moan with pleasure. "Shit . . . Ryder . . . mmm." I can feel my entire body come alive with every touch, the cold from the rain forgotten as warmth spreads through me. He starts to suck faster, with his hand jerking me at the same time. I moan louder, "Ryder! Mmm . . ." I bite my lower lip, trying to stifle my noises as I let myself feel everything.

He pulls off, his hand still working my length. "God, you sound so fucking sexy moaning my name."

"Ryder . . ." I moan softly as dips back down.

"Mm-hmm," he groans, his mouth filled with my length. Warmth is swirling in my core and I can feel sparks as he brings me closer to coming. But I don't want to come in his mouth, no matter how good this feels.

"Come here . . ." I grab his arm and pull him off me, bringing his face up to mind. I lean into his ear and whisper, "Fuck me . . . now."

He pulls away slightly, looking in my eyes as if he's determining how serious I am. "We don't have to do it here, baby," he says. "We can do it where it's more comfortable."

"This is the perfect place. I want to give you everything and more. I want to belong to you. Make me yours, please."

Ryder smiles at me and kisses my forehead "Lay on your side we can take it slow okay?"

I nod and do what he asks me to do. I feel him next to me. He kisses the back of my shoulder comforting me, "You ready, baby?"

"Yes please . . . fuck me."

"Mmmm . . . I love hearing how desperate you are for me." Ryder says. I hear him lick his fingers before he reaches for my hole. He massages with a firm but soft pressure.

The moment I feel his finger sliding in my ass I let out a loud gasp.

"I'll take it slow . . . tell me when it's too much. I got you."

I feel another finger rub my hole making me moan louder. He slowly enters my tight hole with his finger stretching it out for his cock. I moan as I feel myself get wider with each finger he adds.

"Baby . . . please fuck me!" I grunt, his fingers make me want to cum all over him.

He kisses my shoulder as he pulls his finger out. He quickly reaches for his wallet, opening it to grab a condom and a small lube packet. I smirk at him.

"Prepared, aren't we?"

"Hey, always be prepared." He laughs leaning forward to kiss me softly, anchoring me to this moment. "You ready?"

"More than ready." He puts the condom on and rubs the lube on my hole slowly.

He gets closer to me, and I feel his hard cock rub against my hole. I gasp as the tip slides up between my cheeks.

"Fuck . . ." I moan.

"Take a deep breath for me . . . it's going to hurt a little before it feels good. You can trust me, baby."

"I know I can."

I take a deep breath in, and he slides his cock in me slowly. I feel myself stretch even more than I did with his fingers.

"Ah . . . shit . . ." I grunt.

Ryder slows down, "You okay? Should I stop?"

"No! Keep going, I want more please . . ."

He pushes himself in me, inch by inch. I feel his cock throb inside me.

"Fuck! You're so warm and tight . . ." Ryder groans. "I don't know how long I can last."

"Harder. I need it harder, baby. I can take it," I say. Without a word, Ryder goes in deeper. Long thrusts in and out of me. His length hitting all the right places. "Yes! Fuck! Ryder! Ah . . ."

Ryder reaches over to grab my hand, taking it with his. We use the car window to steady ourselves. "God, you feel amazing! Fuck! I wanted this for so long. You're mine forever, Leo."

Ryder slaps my ass as he fucks me hard and I start to jerk myself off with my other hand, wanting to cum with him. I grind into him, moving with his body, making his dick hit my g-spot.

"Mmmmm . . ." I moan. "Cum in me, Ryder. Mark me as yours."

With those words, Ryder lets out a raspy moan, "Fuck! I'm cumming .
. shit . . . mmm."

The sound and feel of him coming undone makes me cum instantly. His
warm cum fills the condom up with each pulse. I'm his and he is mine. We
lay there breathing heavily coming down from the high of our orgasms, his
cock still hard inside me. I grab his hand and kiss it softly.

"That was fucking perfect. I wouldn't change it for the world."

He slides his cock out of me, making me turn to face him.

"I love you, Leo."

I look into his blue eyes "I love you, Ryder."

Chapter Twenty-Five

Ryder

Leo and I have been inseparable since the night of the ball a week ago. My apartment has never felt more like a home than when he is with me. Leo has taught me so much about life and what I want for our future. The only time we don't get to see each other is when we are working and the best part is, when the night is over, we meet in the middle of the crosswalk to hold each other.

Right now, that's all I'm looking forward to after my shift tonight. Leo's working from open to close so he will most likely want to head to my place to sleep. I have no problem with him staying over because I get to sleep with him in my bed. Day by day I wonder more often what life could be like with him living with me.

After the first time Leo stayed over, I knew I wanted to ask him to move in with me. The relationship is fairly new for us, but after a few months, I know where I want it to go.

I check the clock on the wall, waiting for it to hit eight o'clock. I have about thirty minutes till closing, giving me about an hour till I get to see Leo. I planned a little surprise date for us later tonight, so I've got to set that up before the shop closes.

It's a little after nine as I start to set up candles around the coffee bar, along with some barista essentials. Set to one side are the coffee mugs I got printed with the first letters of our names on them. Tonight, Leo will be my barista and I'll be his customer. I've had this date in mind for a while, and I wanted to do something cute for our three-month anniversary. With the holidays coming up I want him to know where I stand in our relationship. We've only been officially dating for about a few weeks now, but I count the moment we met in September as the start of our journey together.

I give the shop one last look of approval, then notice the lights are turning off in the window across the street—my signal to head outside. I dim the lights making the glow from the candles romantic. As I open the door, I see Leo locking up the store's door and he turns around to find me watching him. I instantly smile as my body gets a rush of happiness with each step we take towards each other.

"Hey there, stranger," Leo says, the moment we meet in the middle.

I go in for a hug and he lets me embrace him tightly. I take in his smell and the way his body feels on mine "Hello, my love."

"You okay, Bean?" Leo wanted to come up with a cute name for me since he felt like 'baby' was my name for him. Bean was the first thing he thought of because of my love for coffee, and I fell in love with it.

I moan softly from the back of my throat and nod, "Just missed your touch that's all, babe."

"Well, you have all night to feel my touch, and best believe I want my hands all over you," Leo says, smirking as we pull away from the hug. "Are you ready to go?"

"About that . . . I have a surprise for you! Cover your eyes with this blindfold!"

"The blindfold? Again?"

I chuckle and take Leo's hand to lead him to the sidewalk on my side of the road. "It's three months since the day we met," I explain as I stop him, pulling the blindfold out of my pocket, and lifting it to his face "and I wanted to do something to remember it by. Now give me your hand so I can guide you to where we are going." I lead him to the coffee shop and open the door, "Watch your step, baby."

"I didn't get you anything!" he says quickly.

"Don't worry baby, you being here is all I need." I promise, with a smirk he can't see.

"Ryder, what did you do?"

"You're about to see, but first I need you to use your five senses."

"What do you mean by five senses? Like hearing, touch, taste, smell, and sight?" Leo's face is wrinkled in confusion above the blindfold, but he's going along with my plan.

"Exactly! Now for the first one . . . Hearing. What do you hear?"

"I hear your voice . . ."

"And . . ."

Leo takes a moment to focus on the sounds around us, then adds, "Cars outside . . . My heart beating . . ."

"Perfect. Now, touch. What do you feel?"

Leo reaches out blindly to my shoulder and trails his hand up to my cheek, making me smile softly and lean into his touch slightly. "I feel your warm skin on mine," he says and smiles in my direction.

"Good . . . now what do you taste?"

"I—"

Before he can answer, I step into him, sliding one hand around the back of his head and give him a long, slow, passionate kiss. The kiss takes me back to when I first felt his lips on mine, that day at the bridge. It's soft and gentle, with so much love. I finally pull away to let him answer the question.

"I-I taste you," he says and bites his lower lip, making warmth coil in my core.

"Now, what do you smell?"

Leo takes a few deep breaths, his brow crinkling again. "I smell coffee beans and . . . cookies!"

"You got a good sense of smell, baby" I say, giving him a soft kiss on the nose.

He giggles, "Is it time for sight now?"

I smile as I go behind him to untie the blindfold, "You ready?!"

"Born ready!"

I kiss the back of his neck as I let the blindfold fall off his face to the floor. He takes in the space with all the candles and flowers. My heart is filled with so much love, but butterflies dance in my stomach as I wait to know how he feels. "Baby?" Leo turns around, and I see tears falling down his face. "Oh, baby! I'm sorry—did-did I do something wrong? I can fix it!" I stammer, my stomach sinking.

"No, no," Leo smiles despite the tears. "Ryder, this . . . all of this is so amazing. Thank you!" With that, Leo crashes his lips onto mine, showing me how much this means to him.

I break thee kiss and say, "There's more!" but then duck in for another kiss, before finally easing off. "I got you a barista apron so we can do some latte art!"

"No way!" He turns around and walks to the counter, where a new apron sits in a basket with a few bookmarks for him I made with pictures of us.

Leo reaches out to touch the apron, then picks up a bookmark. "Bean, this is too much—you didn't have to."

"But I wanted to. You mean a lot to me, Leo. You've shown me how much you've grown in the last few months. You deserve to know that I see it."

Leo looks at me with his beautiful brown eyes. "God . . . I love you so fucking much. Our next date I'll be planning, okay?"

"I love you, too and that sounds perfect," I say with a smile. "Now let's get this apron on!"

I help him tie the apron on and let him settle at the coffee machine.

"So, what is my first step?"

I stand beside Leo to explain "Let's pick a type of milk you want to use. When choosing the milk you need to think about the type it is. You want thick and creamy milk, like whole or oat milk, that's easy to froth. Steaming the right type of milk is key to making a good drink."

"Mmm . . . I do like creamy milk." Leo says, giving me a smirk.

I snort a laugh, exclaiming, "Oh god . . . shut up! Focus on the milk, baby."

He bumps my shoulder, but says, "Let's do oat milk!"

As I guide Leo through the different steps of making a latte with the big machine, I end up wrapped around him from behind. And maybe I'm just as much a distraction as I am instructor, with the way my arms wrap around his shoulders as I show him how to hold the milk frother. The way

I drop kisses on the back of his neck as he packs in the ground coffee beans. The way I hold his hips and grind my groin against his jean-clad ass while he lines up the espresso cups.

We get as far as perfectly frothed milk, and fragrant tiny cups of espresso, before Leo snaps.

With a quick swift motion, Leo turns off the steamer and turns, one hand pulling on the back of my neck as we crash our lips into one other. The kiss sends waves of heat all over my body and straight to my bulge.

"What about the drink?" I say, in between kisses.

"The drink can wait," he murmurs, and giggles softly.

Leo leans into the kiss, grabbing my hair as he bites my bottom lip. I move my hand to his neck and gently squeeze it keeping him in one spot so I can kiss him more.

"Fuck . . . Ryder . . . I need you" Leo moans softly as I bite and suck on his neck.

I break off, panting, and say, "We can head home—" Before I can finish my sentence, Leo pulls away and gets on his knees in front of me. "Baby, you . . ."

Leo looks up, his eyes darkened with desire, and I nod as he unbuckles my belt and pulls the front of my boxers down. My erection is met with his lips as he sets it free, sending a raspy moan out the back of my throat that turns into a strangled groan as he takes me into his mouth. Seeing Leo sucking my cock has to be the sexiest sight I've ever laid my eyes on. I grab the back of Leo's head with one hand, holding it steady, my other hand gripping tightly onto the edge of the counter as I thrust into his mouth. He shifts slightly and relaxes his throat, so that I'm making him deep-throat my length with every thrust.

"Shit! Baby . . . fuck. You feel so goddamn good!"

I slow down my pace, giving Leo control on what to do next. He pulls my dick out of his mouth, holding it in one hand as he starts kissing down the shaft down to my balls. Sucking them into his mouth, making me have to steady myself on the counter again.

"I'm gonna . . . I . . . baby!" I moan incoherently.

Leo pulls off me with an audible pop. "Cum on my face, Bean. I want all of you!"

I grab my throbbing cock and start to jerk it off.

"Mmm . . . give me that cum!" Leo moans and opens his mouth, waiting for me to finish on him.

I keep thrusting in my hand, getting closer and closer to the edge. The heat in my core rises to the head of my cock. I focus my eyes on Leo's, looking up at me, and in that moment everything in me is undone as I cum ropes on his face and mouth.

"Ah! Fuck! Baby . . ." I cry out as I ride the high of my orgasm.

"Mmm . . . you taste so good, Bean," Leo says as he licks my cock clean and tucks me away. He comes up from his knees, wiping my cum off his face to lick it off his fingers.

I chuckle, trying to think straight, "You amaze me every time you do that."

"Good, that's my job, right?" he says, winking at me. "I'm going to clean myself up a little then we can get back to that drink. I'll be right back, handsome." He gives me a soft kiss before heading to the bathroom.

I get myself together and start to clean some things up. Moving to Mapleton has been the best thing I've ever done and I'm so happy nothing can ruin it.

I hear the front door open and chime. "Oh, we're closed—" I start saying, looking up, and my heart drops. Everything around me comes crashing down. "Haley."

Chapter Twenty-Six

Leo

I WASH MY HANDS and face in the small bathroom, after letting my sexy ass boyfriend finish on my face. I never knew this side of me existed until things with Ryder got heated. All I can think about when he's close is being naked with him and wanting to let him take all the control in bed. I splash my face to wash off the soap and look at myself in the mirror. I see an entirely different person staring back at me, and it's exactly who I want to be. I'm so happy that nothing can ruin it. I dry my hands off and go to open the door, but then freeze as I hear an unfamiliar voice from the other side.

"Ryder, we need to talk," the high-pitched voice says. *Who is Ryder talking to?* I softly open the door just a little to be able to hear what is happening.

"How did you find me?" Ryder says with a shaky voice.

"I've known where you've been for weeks now. Didn't you get my letter?"

"What letter?" I mutter under my breath, gripping the door handle tightly, utterly confused with what is happening.

"I sent it with a blue envelope, letting you know I'll be coming"

"That was from you! How did you even know where I lived?"

"Your father has tabs on you ever since you left. We all gave you space to find whatever you needed to, until I heard that you have been seeing some guy!"

"Can you keep your voice down!" Ryder says quickly, "Have y'all been stalking me?!"

"I'm your fiancée! I should know where you are and what you're doing!"

Time seems to stop as everything I worked so hard to build comes crashing down with one simple word. My heart is pounding in my ears and a wave of nausea rolls over me, my head filling with a fog of questions.

Fiancée?

Who is she?

Why did he lie?

Was this all a lie?

With that question, a horrifying realization sinks in. I was nothing but a placeholder for him—nothing but an ugly lie. I was fooled. I don't want to hear anything more, but I need to know what is happening. Sucking in a stuttering breath, I listen at the cracked doorway.

"No!" Ryder shouts. "I left you! We are nothing, Haley! I left for a reason. I tried to explain it to you, but you wouldn't listen."

"You left because you were too cowardly to face the truth," this woman—this *Haley*—says in her cold, high-pitched voice and I feel like I can see the sneer on her face through the door. "You are your father's son, and you need to live up to that. You are supposed to get married to me, just like he said."

"My father is nothing but a rich asshole who doesn't know what love really is!" Ryder shouts back. "He had no right to marry me off for money!" There's a pause, then Ryder continues at a lower pitch, "Haley, I'm going to say this once and only once. I will *never* go back to California, nor will I marry you. I don't love you. I love someone else, and I belong to him."

She laughs, "And how does he feel about you being *engaged*?" It was silent for a moment in the coffee shop. In the bathroom, I'm holding my breath. "Ah! So, he doesn't know about any of this, does he? Funny how you say you belong to him but have been lying to him all this time."

The room is spinning, and I can't steady myself. I feel so nauseous.

Then the hated voice continues, "Wait till he finds out about the baby."

Baby . . .

Did she say . . . ? That's it! I can't sit here anymore I need to get out of here.

I push the bathroom door open and rush out of the hallway. Coming out into the main part of the coffee shop, I freeze as I see Ryder and a beautiful blond woman looking at me.

"Leo! Please, I can explain . . ." Ryder exclaims, starting towards me, but my eyes are glued to the woman ahead of me. I untie my apron and throw it away from me, then dodge around Ryder and rush out the door, just trying to get as far away as I can, as fast as I can.

"Leo!" I hear Ryder yell, running after me. "She is lying—there is no baby!"

My view of the familiar nighttime street, lit by streetlamps, is blurred and I dash tears from my face as I run. I'm halfway to my car when Ryder grabs my arm, yanking me to a halt and turning me around.

"Please!" he begs. "Let's talk! I never meant to keep this from you! I needed to find the right moment." The light from the nearest streetlamp highlights the tears rolling down his beautiful face, but I'm hurting too much to care.

"Get off me!" I cry, shaking the arm he holds. "You lied! You made me fall in love with you knowing you are supposed to marry someone else."

"I was never going to marry her! She doesn't mean anything to me. You are the love of my life! I can't lose you, please. Let's talk."

I see Haley walk out the coffee shop and stop on the sidewalk, hands on her hips as she watches us. "Ryder, let him go. You need to come back," she calls in that cold voice.

"Haley, fuck off!" Ryder shouts over his shoulder. "Go back to California and leave us alone! Take your lies with you." He turns back to me "Please can we talk."

"You had three months to talk. You choose to keep it to yourself, and that's on you." I rip my arm out of his hand and head to my car.

"Leo, please stay. Ask me anything you want!" he pleads, following me.

I reach my car and turn to face him. Tears are still following salty paths down my cheeks, but now a hot anger is rising in me. "You know what, Ryder? Fuck you! Fuck you for making me open up to you. You made me fall in love with a version of you that isn't even real! All of this"—I motion between us—"is over! You and I are nothing but a mistake!" The loss of something that I thought was real hits me and I rub my chest. "What hurts the most is that you knew my past and you still kept lying, day after day. I can't forgive you for this, Ryder."

I turn my back on him, get in the car and set the keys in the ignition, turning it on. I put the car in drive to get away from all of this but, before I can hit the gas, Ryder gets in front of my car.

"Leo!" he begs, his hands on the bumper of my car. "Please, we can't end like this!"

"Get out of the way! I don't want to talk anymore," I shout through the windshield. My heart is being torn into pieces. So many voices in my head are shouting, and I can't deal with this anymore. I need to leave. "Ryder, get away from the car. I'm leaving!"

His shoulders slump and he backs away from the car. I hit the gas and pull out of the parking lot onto the road. I see Ryder getting smaller and smaller in my rearview mirror. His image turns blurry as more tears well up. I turn back to the road, but as I glance up again, trying to find Ryder in the mirror, I hear a loud siren. I turn my head towards the sound but see nothing but white. For a moment, I can hear my name being shouted from a far distance.

Then everything goes black.

Chapter Twenty-Seven

Ryder

"LEO!!!" I HEAR ECHOING in my head as I sit in the emergency room. My mind replays the accident again and again trying to find different outcomes. Maybe if I fought harder, Leo wouldn't be fighting for his life right now. This is all my fault. I made him get in the car and drive away. I was the one who broke his heart. I'm to blame for everything. I wish I were hit by the truck instead of Leo.

As I stare at the door where I last held Leo's hand, the world around me moves forwards but I feel like time has stopped and I'm moving in slow motion as I wait to hear about Leo.

"Ryder . . ." Haley whispers next to me.

I lift my head and face her. "What, Haley? What else can you say? What else do you need to take away from me?" I spit the questions out bitterly.

"I'm so sorry. I never wanted something like this to happen."

"It happened! The one person I cherish the most is fighting for his life, and it's on me."

"Ryder, you can't blame yourself for this. You couldn't have known that truck was gonna hit him."

I rub my face with both hands, then press the heels of my hands into my eyes. "I could have fought harder . . ." I say softly.

"Ryder, the way you looked at Leo . . ." Haley's voice is softer than I've ever heard it, almost wistful. "You've never looked at me like that. You truly love him, don't you?"

I exhale loudly and drop my hands to look at her. "He's my soulmate," I say simply. "He always has been and I finally found him."

Haley stands up and faces me. "Listen to me, Ryder. You're gonna have to fight hard for this life. You love Leo and I've seen that. I'll get your father off your back for now. Focus on Leo and his recovery because I know he will get through this. It's time for me to leave, but I'll checkup soon, okay?"

"Okay . . ." I whisper and I watch Haley walk away. It feels like a heavy weight is on me and I bend forward on the uncomfortable hospital chair and drop my head into my hands.

"Ryder!" I hear a shout and lifting my head I see Nina run down the hallway, with Leo's parents behind her. As soon as we got to the hospital, I had called Nina to let her know what had happened. Now I rise to meet them, the guilt chewing me up inside.

When Leo's mom gets to me, she pulls me into a hug. "Honey, are you okay?" she asks with tears in her eyes. She should be worried about Leo, not me.

Wiping a tear from my face, I blurt out, "I'm not okay. This was all my fault."

"What do you mean, your fault?" Nina asks, confused.

"We got into a fight. He found something out that I hadn't had the chance to talk to him about . . ." I start to lose what little composure I had. "He rushed out of the shop and got in his car. I tried to stop him from leaving, but I couldn't. I knew he shouldn't be driving that upset. He sped down the street and, out of nowhere, a truck hit the driver's side." My voice cracks. I don't even recognize it.

Leo's Mom cries harder as I continue to explain, "I called 911 and an ambulance came. But, before we got to the hospital, they had to revive him with a defibrillator. I was by his side all the way to that door. They wouldn't let me go any further." I nod to the door my eyes have barely left and break down. Sobbing, I fall to my knees with my head in my hands.

"So it's your fault." I lift my head to see Nina looking down at me. Crying, her hands are balled into fists, her knuckles white. She's shaking as our gazes lock. A moment later, my back is hitting the floor with Nina's arm on my chest as she pummels me with one small fist.

"You did this!" Nina yells. I just lie there.

"Nina! Stop!" Leo's parents plead as they try to pull her off me.

I stare into her eyes filled with anger and sadness.

She's right.

I did do this.

Nina stops hitting me but yells in my face, "I trusted you, Ryder! You were meant to protect him! Isn't that what boyfriends are meant to do?"

I feel numb as those words hit me. "You're right . . ." I whisper.

She weakens her grip and stands up.

"Then why did you—?" she says in a low, shaky voice, as I get off the floor, my head spinning.

Nina is interrupted by the sound of the double doors opening as a doctor comes out in his scrubs. "Family of Leo Blanco?" he calls.

Leo's parents rush past us, "Yes, doctor! We are his parents! How's our son?"

"Please follow me. I think we should talk in private."

My heart stutters as I hear those words. Something is very wrong.

"Right this way, please." The doctor guides us down a hallway that feels like it will never end. I trail after Leo's parents and Nina and, thankfully, none of them question whether I should be doing so. I have tunnel vision, only the end of the tunnel isn't bright. When we finally get to a room that the doctor ushers us inside of, he shuts the door and takes a seat, signaling for us to do the same.

His expression is unreadable as he faces us and says, "What I'm about to say is going to be hard to hear, but I need you all to keep your hopes up." The air in the room tenses up. I'm holding my breath and Mrs. Blanco reaches out to take her husband's hand. "Your son was severely injured from the accident," the doctor continues. "We didn't know what we were dealing with until we got to the surgery table. He had internal bleeding and had a few broken bones. My team and I were able to control the bleeding, but there have been signs of brain trauma from scans we took."

"What does that mean?" Leo's mom says. "Is he going to be okay?"

"It's hard to say when it comes to brain trauma. The brain is our most important organ, and if any trauma affects it, the outcomes are unknown."

"Can you just say what's wrong? Is it a concussion or something?" Nina asks with frustration. "I just want to see him, please!"

"I'm sorry to say that Leo is in a coma," the doctor finally lets out.

Coma . . .

I freeze as the word reverberates around my head. Leo's parents start to cry again at the news.

"What is going to happen to him? How long will he be like this?" Leo's dad asks, one arm around his sobbing wife.

"It's hard to say when it comes to a coma patient. These cases are all different, and we can't know exactly when or if he will wake up."

"What do you mean *if?*" Nina interrupts, her voice rising as she stands. "He is going to wake up! You can't say you don't know!"

Leo's mom stands and reaches for Nina, "Honey it will be okay," she murmurs, and Nina breaks down as she is wrapped in a hug.

Leo's dad turns to me, his face sterner than I have ever seen it. "You need to leave. You are not family."

I stare at Leo's dad, seeing how broken he is over his son. He blames me for this too. I don't belong here. I stand up and turn to Nina, but Leo's mom blocks me from reaching for her. I take a step back and head to the door, leaving as fast as I can.

"Hey!" I hear from behind me, and I turn around to see the doctor following me. "Before you go, I wanted to give you this." He hands me a small bag.

"What is it?"

"It was with Leo when he went into surgery, and we had to take it off."

"Why give me this?" I question.

He grimaces, his eyes kind. "Let's just say, I have a feeling that this should go to you."

"Thank you. Please take care of Leo for me."

"We will. Just remember none of this is your fault. Things like this happen when we least expect it, okay?"

I nod at him, saying, "Okay" but I don't believe him.

I head out of the hospital and then remember that my car is still at my shop. My head is pounding from all the crying. I don't think I could drive even if I had a car here. I call Jenni to let her know what happened and ask for a ride home, but she tells me she is already at the hospital with Nina. That should have fazed me, but my head is spinning so much I don't think twice about anything.

Remembering what the doctor gave me I reach into the bag. I feel cold metal touch my skin, and I know instantly what I'm touching. I pull out

Leo's bracelet that I gave him for his birthday. Everything inside me breaks as I fall to my knees in the hospital parking lot.

"I can't lose him! Please, I can't. He is my everything!" I scream and shout to the night sky. No one answers me.

The smell of coffee greets me as I wake to my head pounding. I'm in my living room, all the lights are on, and, by the sounds of it, I'm not alone. I give my eyes a moment to adjust then see Jenni making breakfast in my kitchen.

"What the fuck are you doing here?" I blurt out. "How did you even get in here anyway?"

"Getting your ass up and back to work is what I'm doing here. We need to talk, Ryder" Jenni says, turning off the burner under a pan of bacon.

"Again, how did you get in here?" I ask, rubbing my eyes as I get up to head to the bathroom.

"I made a copy of your key when you stopped showing up for work." Jenni gets in front of me blocking my way to the bathroom.

"Move."

"No. I'm not moving until you get your shit together, Ryder. It's been two weeks since the accident, and you've been locked up in this trash-filled apartment."

"I'm not leaving until Leo wakes up," I say, pushing past Jenni.

"Ryder," she says in a soft voice. "It's been weeks. You must start thinking about what will happen if he never wakes up."

"When! It's *when* he wakes up!" I yell, turning towards her. "You don't understand Jenni! He is the reason why I breathe! Without him, my lungs feel like they are clasping within me! I can't live life like he isn't alive, fighting to come back!" Tears fall down my face as I let in the fear of possibly never hearing or feeling Leo again.

Jenni reaches to hug me, but I pull away from her. I don't need anyone else's touch other than Leo's. No one can help me right now. All I want is him—no one else. It kills me that I haven't even been allowed to see him.

Jenni seems to sense that this conversation won't go anywhere and backs off from me. "I'm going to go back to the shop. Please try to eat and clean yourself up, okay?"

"Okay." A promise I won't keep.

Another week goes by as I wait to hear anything from Leo's family. After another intervention from Jenni, I finally shower, dress properly, and leave my apartment to try and work at the coffee shop. Leo's parents find me there. They want to talk about how things went that night, and how they were unfair to me. It's a difficult conversation and I'm a mess again afterwards, but I'm glad we had that conversation, especially as they agree to now let me see Leo.

Nina, on the other hand, hasn't talked to me since that night. I start visiting Leo regularly and, whenever I do, Nina ignores me or leaves as soon as I get to the room.

I'm at Leo's bedside when I hear, from behind me, "Sweetie, you doing okay?" Nurse Nikki enters the room for Leo's hourly vitals.

"I'm doing okay," I say, nodding up at her.

"Okay, good. Remember to keep yourself moving. You have been here all day and haven't moved a muscle."

"I know. I just want to be by his side if he wakes up."

"Honey, if anything changes, you'll be the first to know, okay?" she says with a calm tone. "Now go home and freshen up. He will be waiting for you here."

"Yes, ma'am," I say, smiling at her.

I stood up looking at Leo, and I noticed how different he looks. His face seems slimmer and, when I hold his hand, I can feel how being in the hospital this long affected his body. All I want is to hear his voice again. I bend down to kiss him on the cheek feeling how cold my lips are as they touch his skin.

——

As the hot water of the shower hits my skin, I think of moments with Leo. I miss his touch on my skin and his lips on mine. Thanksgiving is around the corner and all I think about is our plans to celebrate together with his family. Now they were taken away from us because of my mistake.

I lay my head on the shower wall letting the hot water run over my nape. I started to let my mind wander to the moment when Leo and I had sex for the first time. From the way his lips were kissing mine, to the way my hands grabbed every inch of his ass. I feel myself get harder as I think about the moment I slid my cock in his ass. I moan softly as I guide my hand down my abs to my shaft. Feeling it as it throbs in my hand, needing a release. I let my mind take me back to that moment, shuttling my hand back and forth, the motion sending electricity and heat all over my body.

"Leo," I moan softly.

I lay my other hand on the wall to keep me steady as I increase the speed of my hand, letting out more grunts and moans. My eyes are closed as I picture that scene in the car, Leo's body under mine.

"Fuck, Leo!" I grunt.

My body starts to tense up and I groan loudly as my orgasm hits me. I feel the warm cum shoot out of my dick, hitting the wall. The rush from my orgasm is mixed with raw emotions and I let out a scream and slump to the floor of the shower. Tears rush down my face, with water still hitting me. I moan, but it's a moan of sadness that is calling out for Leo. I break and feel myself falling apart as I sit in the shower trying to just breathe.

Then my phone on the vanity rings and brings me out of my head. I quickly turn off the shower and grab my towel. I pat myself dry and tap on the phone screen. I have ten missed calls and a text message. I click on the text message.

[Jenni: Ryder! You need to come to the hospital now! Leo is awake!]

My heart starts racing as I grab what clothes I can find, trying to get myself together. I run out of the room, grabbing my keys, and head to my Jeep. As I drive to the hospital, I'm barely focusing enough to be safe. I just want to get there as fast as I can. When I arrive, I find the closest parking spot and sprint into the hospital, following the now familiar corridors to Leo's room.

Jenni is standing outside. "Ryder! Wait, you—"

"Let me through! I need to see him!"

"Ryder, you need to listen!" Jenni says, trying to get my attention, but it doesn't work as I push her aside. I head into the room and I see Leo's parents sitting next to the bed, but my eyes lock with two beautiful brown eyes. How I've missed those eyes. I feel my entire body finally taking a breath, after weeks of being unable to breathe properly. I take a step towards the bed.

"Ryder," Leo's mom says softly.

"Ryder, we need to talk. Outside, now," Nina says, coming into the room after weeks of no contact, grabbing my arm, about to pull me away.

"But I need to—" I turn my face to Leo and break off at his look of confusion.

"Mom, who is that?" he asks, looking at me.

"Wait? What?" I let out, my pulse thundering in my ears.

Leo's mom looks at me with teary eyes. I head to the other side of Leo's bed, bending down to meet him eye-to-eye.

"It's me. Ryder. Your boyfriend."

Leo looks at me blankly. "Boyfriend? I don't have a boyfriend. Who are you?"

My entire body goes numb.

Chapter Twenty-Eight

Leo

I open my eyes, and everything is so bright that it takes me a minute to register what's around me.

"Doctor! He's waking up!" I faintly hear.

I feel pain all over my body as I get all my senses back. My head seems to be in a fog that I can't escape. I see two figures rush towards me, and I don't realize until they are closer that it is my parents.

"Papi! Are you feeling okay?" My mom says to me, reaching in to hug me.

"Give the boy some space, my love." I hear my dad say, pulling my mom off me.

"We are so happy that you are awake, Leo! These three weeks have been so hard" my mom says to me.

"What do you mean three weeks? I just saw you this morning. Where am I?" I look around the room seeing all the medical equipment. I look at my parents who seem to be worried. "Why are we at the hospital?"

My mom just looks at my dad, her lower lip quivering. My dad sits on the bed and reaches for my arm. "You've been in an accident. You were rushed to the hospital for emergency surgery. When we got here, the doctors told us that you were in a coma. It's been three weeks since your accident."

This can't be real. My head is spinning and feels foggy. I don't understand what is happening. "An accident? I was just with you at home this morning, this doesn't make sense," I say, as I try to move, to sit up. My body doesn't respond normally and pain rolls through me, making me wince and collapse back onto the bed.

My parents share concerned glances, and my mom rushes out of the door, calling for a doctor.

Someone else steps into the room and I glance up to see my bestie in the doorway. "Nina?" I ask. She walks into the room without saying anything and stands at the end of the bed, looking down at me, biting her lip. "You okay?"

Neens starts to cry, "I was so scared to lose you, Leo. Not having you these last few weeks has been so hard!" She quickly comes to me and hugs me.

I'm so confused but pat her back weakly. Then there's a knock on the door, and a very handsome doctor walks in with my parents. I would get a sexy ass doctor as I look bad in this hospital bed.

"Hello, Leo. I'm extremely happy to see that you're awake. I would like to run a quick test. Is that okay with you?"

"That's fine with me."

He raises the end of the bed with a remote, so I'm half sitting up, then produces a tiny torch from a pocket. "Perfect, now can you follow this light with your eyes."

I'd do anything this doctor asks me to do. I follow the light as he asks me a question.

"Leo, can you tell me what day of the week it is?"

"Umm . . . it's Tuesday. I think. Today I have a shift with Neens, and we need to set up the blind book date wall."

My parents and Neens look at each other with concern, making me think something is wrong.

"Perfect. Thank you for following the test, Leo. Now get some rest, okay? Things will make sense soon." The doctor turns to face my parents. "May I talk to all of you out in the hallway?"

My parents and Neens nod and tell me they will be right back, following the doctor out of the doorway.

The more I try to understand what is happening, the more I get this feeling of wrongness that I can't shake off. It's like I'm missing something, but I don't know what that something is. Everyone comes back into the room, looking serious, and gathers around my bed.

My mom sits beside the bed and grabs my hand. "Leo, I need you to know how happy I am that you're awake. It seems that you have amnesia. The day that you described was almost three months ago."

"That can't be right," I exclaim, my voice rising. "Nina, tell them that's not right. How could I forget all that time?"

"Your accident caused brain trauma, that we caught when taking your CT scan," the doctor explains, standing at the foot of the bed. "By the time we could do anything you went into a coma. A brain injury can go many different ways. Losing memories is one of those ways."

"Oh," I say, trying to calm myself, trying to understand what he was saying, my mother's hand gripping mine an anchor in the chaos.

"Let's give Leo some time to rest," the doctor suggests. "I'll be back a little later to check on you, okay?" With a quick smile at everyone, he leaves the room.

"I'm going to step out for a little," Neens says. She follows the doctor out the door and, before the door closes, I see her hug a beautiful girl who seemed to be waiting for her.

"Who's that?" I ask my parents.

"She is a friend of Nina's, but honey, we need you to focus on yourself right now."

"What do you mean friend? Do I know her? I have the right to know!" I say, my voice rising with agitation again.

"Leo, we can talk about everything when you are ready," my dad says calmly. "You just woke up, and we want you to get better. That's all you should focus on."

I understand what they are saying, but I just want to know what is missing. I lay back on the bed and stare at the ceiling, trying to piece everything together, but my mind goes blank. I start to hear voices right outside the door, Neens calling out to someone, and I look towards the door as a guy rushes into the room.

"Ryder," my mom says with a warning tone in her voice.

How does my mom know him? Why do I suddenly feel extremely warm?

Neens quickly enters the room pulling on the cute guy's arm, "Ryder we need to talk. Outside, now."

Ryder...

"But I need to—" he says as he stares at me, his blue eyes bright and glazed with unshed tears. I don't understand what I'm feeling. I'm confused by everything around me. What I do need to know is who this man is.

I look at my mom, "Mom, who is that?"

I notice his face change when I say that.

"Wait? What?" His face loses all emotion.

He looks at my mom to find answers, but he seems impatient and he walks round to the side of the bed. Bending down next to me, he looks into my eyes. I feel this weight on me as he looks into my eyes. I feel my heart beating faster every moment his eyes stare into my soul. My head feels like it's in a cloud.

"It's me. Ryder. Your boyfriend."

Boyfriend!? What in the hell is the man talking about?

"Boyfriend? I don't have a boyfriend. Who are you?"

Chapter Twenty-Nine

Ryder

As I sit in the doctor's office, with Leo's parents and Nina talking about Leo's memory loss, I replay every moment I've had with him. From the moment I first laid my eyes on him from across the street to the very last touch. They're all gone . . . erased from his mind like I've never happened.

"We aren't sure when or if he will regain his memories. That all depends on Leo," the doctor says, making me focus on the conversation that is happening in front of me.

"So, how do we move forward with all of this?" Leo's mom asks the doctor.

"The best thing is for him to go back to his life and live it. Memories can come back if something around him triggers it. He will be able to go home soon," the doctor says with a reassuring smile. But his words don't reassure me,

"Thank you doctor," Leo's parents say.

As we head out of the room, I feel the world around me crumble. I'm nothing but a stranger to Leo. He doesn't love me.

"Ryder, I know this is hard for you. But, right now, Leo needs to focus on getting better. I think what is best for him is that we give him time to understand what has happened. With that being said, you may need to stay away for a little while," Leo's mom says to me.

"How long do I have to stay away?" My heart can't handle this. "I love him . . . I need him . . ." My eyes water as she pulls me into a hug.

"I'm so sorry," she whispers in my ear.

"Large matcha latte for Kyi!" I hear from the coffee bar as I clean up some tables. Being back at work has helped distract me from trying to stay away from Leo. Staying away from him has been the hardest thing I've ever done in my life. Being so close to him yet I can't act on my feelings. His parents made it clear that they want him to focus on getting better. I have to honor that, especially since I was the one who caused all of this. I lost the love of my life because I lied. I move on to the next dirty table and as I wipe it, I lift my head to look outside the window.

"Ryder, you're staring again," Jenni says behind me.

"I miss him," I say softly, keeping my eyes on the bookstore hoping to get a glimpse of him.

"I know you do. Nina told me that he has been doing well. They still haven't talked to him about you, but he has been asking."

My heart jumps, "Wait, he asked about me?" Then the rest of what she says registers. "Also, what's this whole business with you and Nina hanging out a lot? Don't think I haven't noticed."

"Oh, umm . . . we've gotten closer lately."

"How *close*?" I tease, almost grateful to have something to think about other than Leo and the disaster that is my life.

Jenni blushes, making me wonder if maybe this is more than a friendship. "Yeah . . . back to Leo," she says. "I don't want you to assume he is ready. You need to give him his space to figure this all out on his own."

"It's been almost two weeks!" I exclaim. "Thanksgiving just passed. How long do I need to stay away from him? This is harder than him being in a coma. Knowing he is out there, walking around town, and I can't even talk to him . . . This is killing me, Jenni! I'm tired of not being able to do anything. How is he supposed to remember anything if we can't see each other?"

"I don't know, Ryder," Jenni says and sighs. "All you can do is give him the space he needs."

"Whatever. All of this is bullshit," I grab the dirty coffee mugs and head to the kitchen. "I'll be back, I'm going to throw the trash out."

I grab all the trash bags and head to the backdoor that leads to the dumpster. I start throwing the bags in the dumpster and my mind starts to spin. I let out a scream of frustration.

"You okay?"

I turn quickly to see Leo standing a few feet away from me. My heart instantly jumps out of my chest wanting to land in his hands.

"Oh . . . yeah. I'm okay I guess," I say as I study every inch of him, hungry for the sight of him up close. He's grown out his hair, making his curls look longer and perfect. His eyes are different as well. They don't seem as bright as I remember. His clothes seem to look baggier than before. "What are you doing here?"

"I saw you from across the street, looking out your window," he says.

I feel a sense of ease rolls through me at knowing he was also wondering about us.

He looks nervous though, his hands clasped together in front of him, shifting from foot to foot, unable to hold my gaze. "I have a few questions for you. Is it okay if I ask them?"

"Of course you can. Do your parents know you're here?"

"I'm an adult," he spits out, like this has been a point of contention recently. "They can't keep me from wanting answers and getting them."

For all he says that, he's not quick to ask me anything, pacing back and forth and as I stand there and try to resist the impulse to pull him into my arms. All I want to do is run up to him and kiss him. I know I shouldn't, but a guy can dream.

Then he stops suddenly and looks straight at me. "Was I in love with you?"

I give a soft smile before answering him, "Yes, you were."

"I don't believe you," he retorts. "I wouldn't fall for a guy like you. That is too good to be true."

"What do you mean?" I ask, my brow wrinkling. "You love me."

"Loved. Past tense or whatever," Leo says and I barely recognise the harsh tone of his voice. "Someone like you wouldn't date a guy like me, so this has to be a trick. You're messing with my head, dude. I can't stop thinking about you and what all of this even means. Honestly"—he throws his hands out in exasperation—"I wish you never showed up that day. You should have left me in the past."

"Leo! I could never forget you. You're the love of my life." I start to move toward him, but he holds up a hand to stop me.

"Stop! Do not get closer. This was a mistake. I shouldn't have come here." He turns and starts to walk back to the bookstore.

"Then why did you?" I yell after him.

He stops and I can see his shoulders lift as he takes in a deep breath. Then he faces me and quickly walks back towards to me, closer than he was before. He grabs the collar of my shirt in a fist and I just stand there, my breathing picking up at his proximity.

"Because I needed to know," he says, looking into my eyes.

"Know wha—?" Before I can finish my sentence, his lips are on mine. Heat rises within rushing every nerve into overdrive. I feel Leo ease into the kiss with so many emotions that made me want more. I pull away slightly and kiss down his jaw to his neck, making him grunt under his breath.

Suddenly, he pulls back and pushes me away from him, making me stumble.

"No!" Leo shouts. "Please stay away from me! I can't deal with all of this." He turns around and walks away from me. As I watch him leave, my stomach flutters with butterflies from thinking about where my lips were a moment ago.

"Maybe there's hope," I say softly. And, for the first time since the accident, I smile.

Chapter Thirty

Leo

I SLAM OPEN THE house door, rushing past my parents to my bedroom. Locking the door behind me I let my body slide down to the floor, laying my head on the door. Tears stream down my face as I let out all my frustration in the only way I know how. I feel a knock on the door.

"Leave me alone!" I scream.

"Leo, honey, please let us in. We are worried about you," my mom says to me from the other side of the door. "We want to help you, please!"

I stand up and pace my room, pulling on my hair, trying to get all the noises in my head to stop. I feel myself losing it. "No! I don't want your help! I want to stop feeling so confused!"

"We understand, Leo. Please."

"No, you don't! You could never understand what I'm going through!" I yell out. Something takes over me and I start smashing things in my bedroom. Throwing whatever is close to me. Trying to feel something other than anger and sadness. It doesn't help. I fall to my knees and hold my head in my hands and scream, "I can't take this anymore!"

I collapse on the floor and keep crying until I feel myself start to fade to sleep. As my eyes got heavier, I let myself think about the one thing my heart has been calling out for.

"Ryder" I say softly as my eyes close shut.

I stare at the ceiling trying to find a way to get myself out of bed. I haven't left my room since locking myself in four days ago. My parents have only seen a glimpse of me as I went to the bathroom. Every time, before they could talk to me, I was right back in my bedroom. This is the only place I feel some sort of calm, but I know I have to leave this room sooner or later.

I won't remember anything if I lock myself away.

The biggest mystery of my memory loss is Ryder, and I need to find out more. I just haven't been able to build up the courage since that day behind his coffee shop. I felt so stupid letting my emotions take over and kissing him like that. That kiss confused me even more, and now, I'm worse off than I was before seeing him. Something about him has my body on overdrive, and I don't understand all these feelings.

"Ugh!" I grunt, grabbing my pillow to cover my screams of frustration.

I get up from the bed and start to get dressed. I probably need a shower but I desperately need to get out of here suddenly. I don't know where to go, but at least I'll be out of this room.

Leaving my bedroom, I find my parents sitting in the living room, both facing me with anxious expressions as I enter the room.

"Leo! Thank god! We thought you would never leave," my mom says as she rushes to hug me. At first, when she hugs me, I just want her to let go, but after a few moments, her hug starts to feel good.

"Well, I'm out now," I comment, "and I'm going to go for a walk. If that's okay with you guys?"

My dad walks up to us, smiling, "That sounds like a great idea. Would you like us to come with you?"

"No. I think I need to just clear my head on my own."

My mom smiles softly at me "You sure? We wouldn't mind honey."

"I'm positive." I smile back at her. A rush of affection and gratitude hits me and I grab both my parents in a hug. "I love you," I mutter hoarsely, all too aware of how much I've put them through recently.

"We love you more," my dad says, patting my back.

I head out the door, not knowing where I'm going, but just following an instinct. As I walk through Mapleton, I look at it with fresh eyes, seeing all the new decorations and even stores I don't remember. Our little town is thriving, a mix of the familiar and the pleasantly new all around me. My heart starts to feel the warm sense of belonging that I've missed so much. This town has been my home my entire life, and without it, I don't know who I am.

I stop at a crosswalk and look up, realizing that I'm right in front of the bookstore. I must have walked here on autopilot. I take in the view of the bookstore, remembering all the memories I have of being there with my parents and Neens. I turn my head to look at the coffee shop across from me. Unknown feelings rise within me as I try to remember anything about that shop or Ryder. It's like there is a brick wall in my mind that stops me from escaping an endless maze of nothingness. I shake myself out of my head and start to walk again, passing the road where the accident happened. I keep passing through town, taking in every sound and smell. I pass the ballroom where they have the annual ball each year. I was told I went this year, but that was during the period of my memory loss.

The sun is starting to set as my feet lead me into the park. I see the bridge in the distance, and I remember the core memory that has shaped me into who I am today. When I was younger, I would come to this park and play all day long. It was my safe place. One day I was running around, not paying attention to what I was doing, and I fell hard on the ground, twisting my ankle so I couldn't get up. As I sat there, crying from the pain, a boy walked up to me asking if I was okay.

When I first saw him, I felt this rush of emotions that I couldn't explain. He helped me get off the ground and checked on my ankle. The way my skin reacted to his touch had me confused, but I didn't want him to stop. However, that moment didn't last long as he left after helping me. I didn't know who he was, and I'd never saw him in school. This town is small so I would have been able to find him, but he was nowhere to be found. Years later when I started to develop these feelings for boys that everyone said I should have for girls, I remembered that moment. At that time, I was too young to realize what a crush was. He was the first boy I ever noticed, or ever did anything to show they cared about me. I think I could have come to care for him, and he for me. I come back to this bridge when I need to recharge and remember that moment. To remind me that people can care about me and that I could find love someday.

As I get closer to the bridge, I notice a person leaning on the railing, looking out to the waterfall, and then I realize who it is. "Ryder?"

He turns his head to face me, and I can tell he is shocked to see me here. I want to know why he would be here in all places. The one place I've always come to, growing up. This is my place, not his.

"Leo," he says finally, exhaling my name as if he has taken a deep breath for the first time in a while.

Chapter Thirty-One

Ryder

A COOL BREEZE HITS my face as I lean on the railing, looking out at the waterfall, and take in the sky. Watching the sky change from a beautiful orange mixing with a tint of purple as the sun sets sends a calming feeling through me. I started to go back to the bridge to feel more connected to Leo. I've dreamt about seeing him here for many nights, but he never came.

After that kiss a few days ago I've been wanting to go see him, but I wanted to respect his and his parent's wishes. It's been hard to stay away knowing Leo is across the street from me. This entire situation sucks, and all I want is for him to be in my arms again. I just want to see him again.

I hear footsteps coming towards the bridge, but I don't bother to turn my head.

"Ryder," I hear from a voice I know all too well.

Turning my head suddenly, I find Leo standing a few feet away from me. I'm shocked that my dreams are finally coming true. But now I need to know what brought him here. Does he remember me?

I take a deep breath, feeling the air rush into my lungs, "Leo," I say softly.

"What are you doing here, Ryder?" he says with a harsh tone.

"Your parents called me," I explain gently. "They told me what happened a few days ago, and that you went out to clear your head. I knew exactly where you would go. This place is our spot, so I knew to come here."

"No!" He shakes his head furiously. "This spot is *mine*. You are so *suffocating*! You are everywhere I go."

"I'm sorry," I say, trying to stay calm as I turn towards him, "but this is our spot. This is where we had our first kiss. This is where I declared my feelings to you. This bridge means everything to me, Leo."

His anger starts to fade away as he looks away from me and stares at the sky. I wait to see what he will say, but I see tears coming down his face. I step towards him, wanting nothing more than to wrap him in my arms.

"Hey," I say softly, touching his arm to get his attention, "What's wrong?"

He looks down to where my hand is and back up to me. I look into his beautiful brown eyes, and I can see the war raging in his head. His curly hair is a mess, and he has bags under his eyes, making me wonder if he is sleeping. The man I love is falling apart, and there's nothing I can do.

"I-I just want . . ." he says quietly.

"What do you want?"

Leo grabs me and pulls me into a tight embrace, "You."

I feel myself crumble as he holds me. I've wanted to hear this for so long and now that I have, my heart can't slow down, "Leo, I love you. I never stopped loving you."

"I don't understand any of this. Why do I feel so close to you, but I don't know anything about you? You are the first thing I think about when I wake up and the last thing when I go to bed. You've been all I could think about for weeks. I can't take this anymore. I just can't."

"Baby . . ." I breathe, pulling away enough so that I can take hold of his chin and look into his eyes, "I'm right here. You can ask me anything you want. We don't need to rush into anything. All I want is to be close to you."

He meets my gaze and, after a moment of silence, nods. "I would like that," he says, as he rubs tears off his face. "Can we sit down and talk for a little?"

I smile and nod, letting him know I would love to. We sit down on the bench nearby and just sit in silence, watching the sky change into different shades. My heart beats a mile a minute having him right next to me. I might be watching the sky—as he is—but I'm hyperaware of the man next to me. I don't want him to get scared and I resolve to let him navigate where this will go, taking in the moment as much as I can.

"Why are you here?" Leo asks.

I turn my head to him, "Huh?"

"Why are you here, in Mapleton?"

The question catches me off guard for a moment trying to figure out what he meant. "Do you mean why I moved here?"

"Yes."

"Oh . . ." I look back out to the sky, "Well, it's actually a special memory of mine. When I was younger my family and I were going to visit family members in West Virginia, but our car broke down. We ended up in Mapleton and stayed until we could get the car fixed. I went exploring and I came across this bridge. I loved how this place made me feel. The energy around me was so peaceful and inviting, all I wanted to do was stay here for the rest of my life. But I knew I couldn't stay long. On my way back to find my parents, I saw a boy trip and hurt himself. I ran up to him and when he lifted his head something in me clicked. I can't explain it, but it felt like—"

"Love." Leo says quickly.

I turn to him, taken aback by his response. "Yeah! Something about the boy changed me. After leaving Mapleton I knew deep down that I belonged here, and I thought that maybe that boy would be all grown up and waiting for me. When I got here, I didn't have much to go by to find him. Then I met you and everything made sense. At the time I didn't realize, but all I needed was to find you."

Leo is still facing the sky as I try to figure out what he is feeling after hearing my story. He stands up and walks to the edge of the bridge.

"Leo?"

"You know that boy you were talking about?"

"Yeah? What about him?"

"He was me," he says, turning around.

Realization hits me. "Wait, what?!" I say, getting up to face him.

"I was the one who got hurt that day. I remember that day so clearly, like it was yesterday. That was the day I knew I was different. I think I started to fall in love with you that day. I've been in love with you in some way ever since."

I'm speechless. This entire time he has been with me. He was the reason why came back to Mapleton. It's been Leo. It's always been Leo.

"It's you. Leo, you're the reason my heart was left behind that day. It's been with you this entire time. I can't believe this."

"Ryder?" Leo walks towards me.

"Yeah?"

"Kiss me." He grabs my shirt to pull me into a kiss.

The kiss is slow and passionate. We take our time to take each other in. My hand glides up his arm, and up his neck to the back of his head. I wrap my fingers in his curls making him move his head a little so I can deepen the kiss. I hear a soft moan slip from his lips, sending the perfect shivers down my spine. This man is my universe, and no one can change that.

Finally, we pull away, taking a moment to breathe. I lay my forehead on his and we take in air together, our breaths slowly and syncing. Our hearts beat as one.

"I have something for you," I say breathlessly. I reach into my pocket to grab his silver bracelet.

"What is that?"

"This is the bracelet I gave you when we were on a date for your birthday. I've been carrying it everywhere I go hoping that one day I could give it back to you. I'm hoping today is that day."

He looks up at me and smiles softly, "I'll be happy to take it."

I smile and hand him the bracelet. The moment he grabs it he looks at the engraving and feels it with his fingers.

"Ahh!" Leo yelps, dropping the bracelet on the ground as he holds his head.

"Leo! What's wrong?"

He squeezes his head as if trying to stop feeling the pain that he is in. Then, all of a sudden, I see his body relax and he puts his hand down.

"Leo?"

He lifts his head up to face me and, when he does, something is different in his eyes.

"I remember."

"What do you mean, you remember?"

"I remember everything, Ryder." He says and I can tell that he is telling the truth by the way his body tenses up.

"Oh my god!" I rush into hugging him. "This is so amazing!"

His body is rigid and I let go to see him crying.

"I remembered everything the moment I felt that bracelet . . . the lies. The heartbreak. The car crash. I remember it all." His voice is hard as he steps back from me.

I reach for him, "Leo, I know what you heard was crazy. I need you to know that none of that is true. Yes, I was supposed to marry her, but I chose to be with you. It's always been you! We met all those years ago for a reason! We can't let that go."

"That's what makes this even harder, Ryder. All this time has passed, but now these feelings are back. You destroyed everything. I gave my all, and you didn't even tell me the truth. I don't know how to get past that."

"Baby . . . please don't let this go." I step into his space, my face inches from his. I feel his breath on my lips, making me want to kiss him.

He looks at me with his beautiful brown eyes and I see his love fade. He lets me pull him into a kiss. Our kiss feels raw and pure. All our love poured into this one kiss. We pull away, "Please—" I start, but he interrupts me.

"I'm sorry," he says, leaving my embrace.

"Leo," I beg, "please don't do this." He grabs my hand and holds it and, for a moment, I think it might be okay as he looks at me. But then, he starts to walk away. As he pulls his hand from mine, my entire world comes crashing down. I'm frozen to the spot. I can't move my body to follow him, it doesn't let me.

"Please . . ." I try to say, but my voice is shaky. I look down and I see his bracelet on the ground. I pick it back up and look back at him.

I watch as the love of my life walks into the night.

The end...
Or is it?

Acknowledgments

I DIDN'T EXPECT THAT in my 2024bingo card, I would become an indie author at the age of 28. Growing up, I created all these different stories about people around me, making my world more magical and special. I never thought of taking those stories and making them a reality in a book. Even now, I still feel like I don't think I'm a writer or a published author. However, if you truly put yourself out there and lean on your support, your dreams can come true.

I want to thank all of you for taking the time to read my debut novel, and hopefully, you will fall in love with the characters as much as I did. Being able to learn that even if you don't look the way that society wants you to, you still deserve love. It's okay to feel you're insecurities and doubts because it makes you human. I had the chance to learn that as I was writing this story.

To my Tiktok community that has been supporting me from day one with all the love and kind words. Every one of you who has followed my journey during my TikTok lives as I wrote this story and watched me freak out trying to make it the best that I can make it. You all have taught me to be brave in my writing and honest about who I am as I write each word down. You caught me through hard moments and were there during the highest moments. For that, thank you with all my heart.

To Lana, who was the person who inspired me to sit down and write this story. You are an inspiration not only to me and my friends but to this entire world of readers. You're honesty and kindness were all over your content and books. Never let your fire dim. To Micah and Lindsey, thank you for bringing my story to life with your talent. You took what was in my head and made them come to life with the purest energy. I couldn't have done this without you both.

To my beautiful Book Worms, what can I say? As I write this all my emotions come out. You three incredible girls mean the absolute world tome. You are this story and more. Your support has never wavered, and it never will. This debut is for us.

About the Author

Esai Sanchez is a Latin-American born and raised in Northern Virginia. An avid reader who loves to share his reading and writing journey with the world. You can find him reading or writing in his spare time. Music has had a big impact on his creative mind. Never did he think that he would become a romance author in his life. Romance stories have been a part of his life on all sorts of platforms, and they drive him to believe in love. That's what this debut is for him, believing in love again. His debut novel, Brewing a Crush, was a story that was created not only for him but for those who feel or look like him to know that love is possible. So many more stories are in the works for this author and for his dream of being an indie author.

Tiktok & Instagram – **Authoresai**

Leave comment about your own love story or how you connected with the book!

Please consider leaving a review on Goodreads, Amazon, etc. Thank you for everything!